Published by Blue Merle Publishing
www.bluemerlepublishers.com
December 2024

ISBN 979-8-9907305-2-6

A Gift from Ladybug Farm:

A Novella by

Donna Ball

Also in this series:

A Year on Ladybug Farm
At Home on Ladybug Farm
Love Letters frm Ladybug Farm
Vintage Ladybug Farm
A Wedding on Ladybug Farm
Christmas on Ladybug Farm
Recipes on Ladybug Farm

A Note from the Author

Dear Reader,

It has been 15 years since *A Year on Ladybug Farm* was published. Six books followed chronicling the adventures of Cici, Bridget, and Lindsay on Ladybug Farm, along with three spin-offs featuring their best friends Paul and Derrick at the Hummingbird House B&B. I could not imagine when I began the series how many lives would be touched by my simple stories, some of them profoundly. I have received multiple letters from mothers and daughters who read the books together, some who were reunited after long estrangements over their love of the books, and some (this makes me cry every time!) whose last moments together were spent reading aloud from one of the Ladybug Farm books. Other readers recounted how the Ladybug Farm books had seen them through tragedies and major life-changing events. Quotes from Ladybug Farm have been printed on mugs and posters, embroidered on tea towels, and turned into internet memes.

Believe me, none of this was my intention, and no one could have been more surprised than I was at how well the books were received. I just wanted to tell a good story and maybe, in the process, make some people smile. I am honored and deeply humbled by how wholeheartedly the ladies of Ladybug Farm have been embraced, and by how vividly they live on in the hearts of readers all these years later.

The last book of the series, *A Wedding On Ladybug Farm*, was released in 2014, Yet not a single week has gone by since then that I haven't received an inquiry about when the next book is coming out. My standard reply has always been, "No further books are planned at this time." There were many reasons for this. I felt that the future of Ladybug Farm had been nicely laid out in the conclusion of *A Wedding on Ladybug Farm. The Hummingbird House, Christmas at the Hummingbird House* and *The Hummingbird House Presents* continued the storyline of Ladybug Farm, though from a slightly different point of view. And I needed to turn my time and attention to other projects, including launching and maintaining three mystery series over the past ten years.

Yet the letters kept coming, and from time to time I found myself wondering what a revival of Ladybug Farm would look like. Was it even possible, after all these years? Ladybug Farm was created in a much kinder, easier time than the one in which we live now. I had to wonder whether there was even a place for the gentle wisdom and biting wit of Ladybug Farm in today's world. Or is the answer to that question, in fact, that we need Ladybug Farm now more than ever?

We are about to find out, You hold in your hands my gift to you, the first installment in the Ladybug Farm saga in ten years. And—get this! —though a decade has passed for the rest of us, through the magic of fiction, barely two years have passed on Ladybug Farm (even though they do, again in magical fiction-land, take advantage of many of the same amenities we enjoy today, like Google translator. Don't try to figure it out). So welcome back to Ladybug Farm! If you enjoy your visit, let me know, because as you've surely realized by now, I do care what you have to say.

With love from Ladybug Farm,

Donna Ball

The Legend of Ladybug Farm

For those of you who are just joining us...

Once upon a time, three best friends named Cici, Bridget, and Lindsay came upon a magnificent old mansion nestled in the heart of the Shenandoah Valley. The house was a neglected mess, with falling down outbuildings and a farm that had gone to weeds. But our three heroines loved a challenge. Their husbands were gone, their children were grown, and they were ready to start the next chapter of their lives. They took on the old house, restoring it to its former glory piece by piece, despite marauding sheep, the caprices of nature, a persistent pet deer, and a cranky nonagenarian housekeeper by the name of Ida Mae Simpson. By the end of the first year they had not only made a home for themselves, but a family, and all of their dreams were within reach.

Well, more or less.

Cici's college-aged daughter Lori came for a visit and showed no desire to leave. Lindsay adopted a homeless teenager, Noah. The ladies' best friends from the city, Paul and Derrick, decided to embrace the country life and bought a Bed & Breakfast six miles away, completely undeterred by the fact that they knew nothing about either running a B&B or living in the country. The ladies of Ladybug Farm survived fire, blizzard and the good intentions of their children and best friends. They were secure in the belief that all will be well in the end, and if all is not well, it's not the end.

Or so they say.

Having tried numerous ways to keep their dream alive—chickens they couldn't bear to harvest, a wedding venue destroyed by a goat—the ladies sank their remaining resources into a desperate attempt to revive the vineyard. They hired a vintner by the name of Dominic Duprey who slowly but surely brought their vision to fruition... while also courting a quite willing Lindsay. Cici's daughter, Lori, who to this point had been nothing if not unemployable, showed a remarkable talent for winemaking and began studying under Dominic's tutelage. Bridget finally saw her dream of opening a farm-to-table restaurant on the premises take shape. Everything was perfect.

Until it wasn't.

Noah, a talented young artist, broke Lindsay's heart and almost tore the family apart by joining the military. Lori, suffering from a painful break-up, ran away to Italy, where she encountered more heartbreak. Bridget's son Kevin was involved in a scandal of his own making and lost his law license. A hailstorm destroyed the newly planted vineyard. It looked as though the dream of Ladybug Farm was over.

And yet...

Lori married Kevin, and the two of them came home to Ladybug Farm to help restore the vineyard and run the winery. Lindsay married Dominic, and the two of them made their home in a folly on the edge of the property. Bridget opened her restaurant in the old dairy barn (*The Tasting Table, open 11:00—3:00 Thursday through Saturday, April 1 through October 31. Tell your friends*). Under Dominic's management, the winery produced its first award-winning vintage. Ladybug Farm became self-sufficient through winery tours and specialized sales. And finally, everyone lived happily ever after.

Well, almost...

One

Another Christmas Party

The house had survived three wars, two fires, twelve tornadoes, a flood, and innumerable blizzards. It had stood solid against generations of feral children with their sharp sticks, finger paints, and various flying projectiles. It had borne witness to fifteen births and twenty-eight deaths, two of them murders. There was very little the old house hadn't lived through. Yet the objective observer could hardly be blamed for wondering whether it could survive one more Ladybug Farm Christmas party.

The exterior of the house was festooned with garlands of greenery studded with white poinsettias and red velvet bows that were draped from one corner of the wide front porch to the other. An eight-foot blue spruce, decorated with red plaid ribbons, garlands of popcorn, and approximately a thousand multi-colored lights stood beside the front door. Beneath it were boxes wrapped with gaily colored Christmas paper, the whole surrounded by a train chugging cheerily through a snowy Christmas village—or at least it did until the farm's resident sheepdog snatched the engine and ran away with it, which happened at least once a day.

Six white rocking chairs dressed in red plaid cushions were lined up against the wall, each draped with a plush Christmas-themed throw, and an enormous fruit-studded wreath adorned the front door. Framing the door was another living garland embedded with twinkling white lights, matching the motif of the tall, lead-paned windows that stood sentry across the front of the house. In each window was a candle, naturally. Woven baskets of cinnamon-scented pine cones and sprays of greenery decorated each wicker end table along the front porch. Nets of tiny white lights illuminated the six boxwoods—three on either side—that led to the front steps, and a pot of bright red poinsettias sat on each riser. Today even nature had cooperated, dressing the scene with three inches of gently falling snow overnight. On the whole, the front porch of Ladybug Farm would not have been out of place in a department store window.

The winter wonderland continued on the interior, with another tall spruce centered under the chandelier, this one decorated in silver and white, with painstakingly constructed velvet and lace ornaments. A heavy cedar garland entwined with silver ribbon and sugared fruit draped the banister of the sweeping staircase, and on the balcony above was another Christmas tree, this one decorated with pink velvet ribbon and white lace angels. In the wide main parlor, a fire danced in the fireplace, and above it was a tall mantle displaying a winter forest scene. Twinkle lights were everywhere, and the entire house smelled like evergreen and cloves. Every corner of the eight-thousand-square-foot old mansion was lovingly, tastefully, delightfully decorated for the season, and every single corner was completely over the top.

In the big country kitchen, Bridget removed another tray of sugar cookies from the oven and placed them on the counter to cool. Lori, thirty-six weeks pregnant with twins and looking every minute of it, sat at one end of the enormous center island—actually a converted farmhouse table—carefully piping decorations onto the cookies that had already cooled. There were evergreen wreaths on every window and on the back door. The stone arch that surrounded the raised fireplace was draped with garland, and the family table that was drawn up before it held a charming gingerbread centerpiece and another eight dozen decorated cookies.

Approximately one-half of the island was filled with cookies waiting to be decorated; the other half held two fully cooked turkeys, a ham, eight foil-covered casserole dishes, a lazy Susan waiting to be filled with appetizers, three dozen miniature pastry shells waiting for their crabmeat filling, three dozen hard boiled eggs ready to be turned into deviled eggs, and two frosted cakes. Marinara sauce simmered on the back burner of the stove and mulled cider simmered on the front burner, filling the kitchen with a complex mixture of rich aromatics. It was three o'clock on Christmas Eve afternoon, and although the main event, which included approximately fifty invited guests, wouldn't begin for another twenty-four hours, the most important guest was expected in less than two.

Noah was coming home for Christmas.

Cici came into the kitchen with her long-legged stride, holding a blank sheet of paper in her hand. She was festive in a red-and-white striped sweater and jeans, her thick honey-colored hair held back with a headband decorated with tiny poinsettias. Her freckled face and quick, energetic manner helped disguise the fact that she was over sixty —though barely over, as she was quick to remind anyone who dared bring up the subject. Not that it mattered because as everyone now knew, sixty was the new forty.

Her brow was furrowed in puzzlement as she waved the paper in the air. "I don't know what's wrong with that printer," she said. She went over to the laptop that was open on the family table beside the fireplace and tapped a couple of keys. "It says 'ready to print' but it won't print. I've tried everything I know." She clicked the mouse a couple of times. "What am I doing wrong?"

Bridget pushed her hair away from her face, which was flushed and damp from the heat of the oven, and held it back with her fingers for a moment to cool off. She had worn her hair in the same blonde bob for thirty-five years and hadn't yet realized that the style might not be the most practical for someone who spent her days putting things in and taking things out of a hot oven. She was a few years older than Cici, petite and round and stylish even in a checkered apron with snowflakes on it and jingle bells dangling from the ruffled hem. The outfit was accessorized, naturally, by red velvet pumps.

She looked worriedly out the window, where snow was still falling in a steady mist. "What do you think about the roads? Will they be okay tonight? You don't think the roads will freeze before he gets here, do you?"

Cici's scowl deepened and she tapped the keys again, more forcefully this time. "I hate things that don't work the way they're supposed to," she muttered, "Come on, you stupid printer. You've got one job."

Lori, concentrating on piping tiny red berries onto a wreath of green frosting, said, "Maybe it's too hot."

Lori was a striking-looking twenty-eight-year-old with porcelain skin, now blotchy with hormones, and beautifully sculpted features, now puffy with eight months of pregnancy. As an homage to Christmas Eve, her cascade of coppery curls was fastened back with holly-wreath barrettes, and she wore a burgundy jumpsuit of stretchy velveteen over a white turtleneck. The outfit had been adorable on her when she was a size 2; now it was so tight it outlined the shape of her belly button.

Bridget looked at her in confusion. "It's thirty-four degrees on the porch," she pointed out uncertainly, "and it's going to get a lot colder before nightfall. The roads always freeze up before the ground does."

It was Lori's turn to look confused. "I was talking to Mom."

Cici glanced at her daughter skeptically. Lori wasn't very good at math, couldn't follow a recipe if her life depended on it, and had been known to mistake a nanny goat for a llama. But if there was one thing she did know, it was tech. Unfortunately, pregnancy brain had begun to assert itself with increasing frequency over the past several weeks, and the other members of the household had learned to think twice before acting on anything Lori said.

Cici explained carefully, "The printer is in the office, which is freezing cold because it has no heat. That's why I'm working here in the kitchen, remember?"

Lori examined the freshly decorated cookie critically, added one more berry, and set it aside with an approving nod. "Not the printer," she told her mother. "The laptop. It's sitting right next to the fire. Microprocessors can overheat, you know. That's why you're not supposed to leave laptops or phones in a hot car."

Cici said, "Oh." She tried to hide her surprise at the fact that the explanation actually made sense, and she quickly moved the computer away from the fireplace. After a moment's indecision, she opened the back door and placed the laptop on the end table beside the porch swing—after first nudging aside a wreathed candle display, of course.

Cici closed the door on the fog of cold air that crept inside and took a bowl of crab-and-cream-cheese filling from the refrigerator. "Do we have another piping bag? I can fill the puff pastries while I wait for the laptop to cool down."

"Butler's pantry, bottom shelf," Bridget said. She came over to Lori, wiping her hands on her apron. "Honey, these are beautiful, but at this rate, you're going to be here all night. Why don't I pipe the wreaths, and you do the berries?"

She held out her hand for the piping bag, but Lori was reluctant to turn it over. "I just want everything to be perfect for the babies' first Christmas."

Cici returned from the pantry with the piping bag in hand, and she and Bridget exchanged a quick look that contained a thousand unspoken observations about the last crazy weeks of pregnancy. Cici had spent the remaining three days before giving birth folding and unfolding doll clothes, Bridget had hidden $5.00 bills all over the house. She was still finding them when her youngest went to college. With all this and more in mind, neither one of them dared point out to Lori that, since the babies weren't born yet, this wasn't *exactly* their first Christmas.

"I'll make perfect wreaths, I promise," Bridget assured her, and Lori reluctantly surrendered the piping bag filled with green icing. Bridget sat down and began to draw quick, efficient circles on the cookies with the icing. "What are you printing, anyway?" she asked Cici.

"The menu for tomorrow's party," Cici replied. She scooped spoonsful of crabmeat filling into the pastry bag and screwed on a tip. "You know we've got all those little easels left over from Lindsay's birthday party a couple of years back, so I thought we'd use them to display the names of the dishes on the buffet table."

"Oh, that's a good idea. I'd forgotten we even had them. Of course, we haven't really done any entertaining since... Well. You know." Her expression, and her tone, fell. She finished quietly, "Since the funeral."

A somber veil dropped over the room, and no one said anything for a moment. Lori stopped piping berries, Bridget looked up from the green wreath she was making and stared determinedly at the crackling fire, blinking hard. Cici pulled out a chair and sat down at the table, but she kept her gaze fixed on the tray of empty pastry shells. In another moment she said softly what they all were thinking. "It doesn't feel like Christmas without her."

"Mom, don't," said Lori gruffly. "If I start crying the frosting will get all soggy." She reached across the table and pointed at one of the cookie wreaths. "That one's crooked."

Bridget managed a smile, banishing the moment with determination, and went back to making wreaths. "Sweetheart, you know the babies can't actually see the cookies, don't you?"

"It's all about intention," Lori asserted. "And if we don't pay attention to the details now how will little Peyton and Paisley ever develop good taste?"

Cici made a dry face and began quickly piping filling into the pastry shells. "Talk to me about details in three months."

And Bridget lifted an eyebrow. "Peyton and Paisley? I thought it was Colt and Cara."

"I liked Colt," put in Cici.

"We're still experimenting with names," Lori said. "I'll know when it's right." She tapped another cookie. "Crooked."

Bridget gave her a hard look and Cici intervened quickly, coming around the table to take Lori firmly by the shoulders. "Let Bridget finish the cookies," she advised, urging Lori to her feet. "You're needed on deviled egg duty. Come over here and start shelling these eggs."

Lori struggled to her feet, groaning loudly and holding on to the back of a chair for support. Her oversized belly always threatened to overbalance her. "Great," she complained, "Now I've got to pee." She grimaced and pressed a hand into her back. "Ouch! One of the little monsters just kicked me in the kidney."

"Probably because he noticed the crooked wreath on the cookie," Bridget muttered under her breath, but not quite softly enough. Lori scowled at her.

A waft of cold air scuttled across the kitchen as the back door opened and Kevin came in, stamping the snow off his boots and carrying Cici's laptop. "What's the laptop doing on the back porch?"

"I couldn't get the printer to work," Cici explained. "Lori said the computer needed to cool down."

Kevin lifted an eyebrow that explicitly said, *And you believed her?* He wisely did not say it out loud, however, as he handed the computer over to Cici. "I think it's cool enough now." He shrugged out of his fleece-lined jacket and turned to hang it on the hook by the door. "Anyway, the reason the printer isn't working is because the Wi-Fi is down. I know because I just tried to check on Noah's flight. You have a Wi-Fi printer. I'll check the router."

Cici stared at him. "The Wi-Fi is down? How could I not check that? That's usually the first thing I check." She rubbed her temple and looked at Bridget uneasily. "Do you think I'm getting dementia? Isn't that one of the first signs?"

"Forgetting to check the Wi-Fi?" Bridget did not look up from her steady, efficient piping. "That's what I heard. The second sign is leaving six dozen puff pastries only half filled with crabmeat filling."

"Right." Cici put the laptop aside and hurried back to her station.

Lori said, "What about Noah's flight?"

"Don't know." Kevin came forward to kiss his wife. "The Wi-Fi is down. And cell service is at its usual peak efficiency. Zero bars." He bent and placed a light kiss on either side of Lori's belly. "How are little Liam and Lesley?"

"Peyton and Paisley," Cici corrected.

"Sheldon and Sherry," Lori corrected her. "And they're both horrible. Every time I move, one of them kicks me and they take turns sitting on my bladder while the other one sits on my kidneys. My back is killing me. Your children are ruining my life. And I really have to pee."

She started to leave the room and Kevin informed her cheerfully, "You knew twins ran in my family when you married me."

She looked back hopefully. "Did you get the nursery painted?"

Kevin was a good-looking young man with thick brown hair, Clark Kent glasses, and a newly acquired beard that he insisted made him look more scholarly, but which did little to disguise the lines of fatigue that were becoming etched into his face. He had once been an up-and-coming lawyer with a prestigious Washington firm, but his life had changed forever when he fell hopelessly in love with the girl next door – whom he only had to travel three thousand miles to meet. He now taught three days a week at the junior college, was the part-time business manager of Ladybug Farms Winery, worked on his PhD at night, and in his spare time was enlarging the former folly at the edge of the property into a two bedroom, two bath cottage where he and Lori—who was the general manager of the winery—could raise their new family. In the meantime, they lived upstairs in the master suite of Ladybug Farm, an arrangement that had been suboptimal for quite some time.

"Almost," Kevin assured her, and anyone could tell he was lying. "But, babe, until the plumber gets here the electrician can't work and until the electrician gets here there's no heat, and without heat, the paint won't dry. I got the last of the sheetrock up, though," he added hopefully.

Cici spoke loudly to cover Lori's angry sputtering, "That's fantastic, Kevin!" she exclaimed. "I'll help you with the painting as soon as the heat is on and we'll have it knocked out in a day."

"—not bringing my babies home to a house filled with poisonous paint gas!" Lori cried. Then, abruptly, "Stay right there, I'm not finished." She hurried out of the room as fast as she was able. "And start shelling those eggs!" she tossed over her shoulder as the door swung closed behind her. "I love you!"

"Love you back," he called. "Not shelling eggs!"

"Good." Cici pulled the bowl of hard-boiled eggs protectively closer. "You always mangle them."

Kevin, taking it in stride, helped himself to a cookie and kissed his mother on the head. "Man, it smells like Christmas in here. Rebel's in the barn," he added, "so nobody has to worry about being mauled when they get out of the car."

Rebel, the farm's resident sheep dog, liked to attack the tires of moving vehicles, and sometimes the occupants of said vehicles. Kevin was the only one who could completely control him.

"You gave him the dog biscuits I made for him,

right?" Bridget said. She paused in her work to give him an anxious look. "And left him plenty of food? I just feel so bad, leaving him in the barn. It's Christmas, after all."

"Mom," replied Kevin patiently, "he's a border collie locked in a barn with twenty-five sheep. This is the best Christmas of his life. The horses aren't wild about it, but they'll get over it. And Peaches wouldn't come in, so I let her stay out there with him." The golden retriever was not an outdoor dog, but she had developed an inexplicable affection for the half-feral border collie and, if given a choice, would take his company over that of her human companions any day.

Cici said, "Why are the sheep in the barn?"

"It's cold," replied Bridget a little defensively. "And it's Christmas."

Cici decided not to follow up on that. Instead, she asked Kevin, "How does it look out there?"

"The same as it does in here," he answered. "Like a Hallmark Channel Christmas movie exploded all over the place."

Bridget gave him a mildly offended look. "This is the first time Noah's been home for Christmas in two years," she asserted. "Of course we want everything to look nice. Anyway, she meant the roads."

"They might get a little slippery tonight," he said, "but they should be fine until Noah gets here." Kevin pulled out a chair and sat down, stretching out his legs as he reached for another cookie. "Anyway, you're talking about a big strong Marine, here. I think he can manage a little bad weather."

Cici said, "Remember the first Christmas party we gave here? There was a blizzard and we didn't think anyone would make it, but everyone did."

"And then Noah showed up," Bridget added, "on a motorcycle!"

"With Lori on the back of it." Cici suppressed a shudder at the memory.

Bridget smiled reminiscently, "Best Christmas ever."

Cici paused in her piping to look at Bridget, and the smallest shadow of sadness flickered across her face. Then she put on a resolute smile and said, "This is going to be a great Christmas, too. Maybe…" She paused for a determined breath. "Maybe there'll be an empty place or two at the table, but we've got our kids…"

"And grandkids," Kevin reminded her.

"Who I think we can all agree are the youngest guests ever at a Ladybug Farm Christmas party," Cici pointed out, making Bridget chuckle.

"And don't forget whatever surprise Christmas present Noah said he was bringing," Cici added.

Bridget's eyes lit up. "I love surprise presents. What do you think it is?"

"Maybe it's a puppy," Cici suggested, knowing that would make her friend smile. "You know how crazy he is about animals."

"Nah," said Kevin, just as Bridget had started to clap her hands together in delight. "He's flying in from Germany. He'd never get a puppy through customs. I think it's a promotion." He took another cookie. "Or maybe a new assignment, closer to home."

"Lindsay would love that," Bridget said wistfully. And then she sighed, "Not that it matters anymore."

Cici, determined to keep the conversation upbeat, said, "Or maybe it's his discharge papers. Anyway, Kevin…" She shook out her hand to relieve a cramp and picked up the piping bag again. "Could you go fix the router, please? And check on his flight."

"And when you get back," added Bridget, "take all of these dishes down to the refrigerator in The Tasting Table. We've run out of room up here."

"Yes, ma'am." He pushed to his feet and winked at Cici, correcting, "Ma'ams."

Cici blew him a kiss. "You're a sweetheart."

Kevin left to examine the router, and as he exited by the left-hand door, the right-hand door swung inward to admit Ida Mae. Ida Mae Simpson was in her nineties (by anyone's best guess, as she refused to admit to her age) with a cap of iron-gray curls and a fierce expression who ruled the household by force of will and a refusal to take no for an answer. She had been keeping house at Ladybug Farm decades before it was even called Ladybug Farm, and had long since become more of a fixture than an employee. She used a cane these days, due to what she called "the misery in my hip," but showed no other signs of slowing down. She marched into the kitchen with a scowl on her face, jerked her head back toward the way she had come, and demanded, "What in tarnation is that girl wearing? That overall's so tight I can see the color of them babies' eyes."

Cici couldn't prevent a chuckle, and Bridget, fighting a smile of her own, said, "Things aren't like they were in our day, Ida Mae. Young women like to show off their baby bumps."

"Or mountain, in Lori's case," Cici murmured, still fighting a grin.

"Well, I think it's indecent."

"They also glam themselves up for labor and delivery," Cici pointed out, mostly to get a reaction out of Ida Mae. "Paul is taking Lori into the city next week for a full makeover so she'll look pretty for the photographer. Hair, nails, makeup, the works."

Ida Mae stared at her. "You think I believe that?"

"It's true," Bridget assured her. "They're even hiring a professional photographer to be in the delivery room and get that first mom-and-baby shot. Paul's gift to them to them, of course."

Ida Mae scowled and grunted, "The craziest thing I ever did hear." Then she raised her cane in a sweeping gesture that included everyone in sight, and demanded, "Out of my kitchen. I got a Lane cake to frost."

Bridget said patiently, "Ida Mae, we have three layer cakes already, not to mention your fruitcake and all these cookies. Don't you think..."

"Not making it for you," responded Ida Mae tartly. She propped her cane against the wall and took her apron off a hook near the stove. "We got a home-coming, ain't we? Lane cake is for homecomings."

Cici, who usually found it best to stay out of these conversations, felt compelled to point out, "Noah doesn't like raisins, and Lane cake is loaded with raisins."

She sniffed and tied the apron over her bulky denim overalls and wool sweater. "Ain't making it for him, either. Now, get on out of my way. My boiled frosting needs time to set before supper."

Cici and Bridget exchanged a puzzled look. Lane cake was an incredibly complex and time-consuming dessert that took at least two days to make. Ida Mae had worked on it all day yesterday, baking the fluffy white sponge, chopping the fruit, making the brandy-infused custard filling, assembling the three-layer cake and letting it sit overnight to absorb the flavors. The whole would be topped with a decadent white frosting that looked as elegant as it tasted. Cici and Bridget loved the cake, but they rarely got more than one slice because it was Lindsay's absolute favorite.

Lindsay's favorite. They both realized it at the same time, and Bridget suppressed a small wince. Cici just looked at her helplessly, not knowing what to say.

"Ida Mae," Bridget said gently, "Lindsay's not here. You know that, don't you?"

Ida Mae answered with a grunt, "Do I look blind to you? How about you get my double boiler down from the top cabinet and then get on out there and take care of your company."

Cici got up quickly and retrieved the bowl for her. "Noah's not due for another hour, at least," she pointed out. "We've got plenty of time."

"Then who do you reckon just pulled up in the driveway?"

Cici ran to look out the window and Bridget sprang from her chair excitedly. "Noah!" she exclaimed. "It's Noah! He's early!"

But it wasn't Noah.

Two

A Christmas Wish

"Darlings!" Paul came up the front steps, brushing snow off the shoulders of his cashmere coat, at a brisk stride. He was a good-looking, nattily-dressed man in his sixties with a head of perfectly coiffed silver hair and the air of someone who was accustomed to being welcomed wherever he went. He and his partner Derrick owned the Hummingbird House B&B, and they had been the ladies' best friends for over two decades. He was followed up the steps of the house by a man and a woman neither Cici nor Bridget had ever seen before.

"A hundred thousand apologies for just popping in like this." Paul opened his arms wide and embraced Cici, air-kissing her cheek—"Mwah!"—And then Bridget, "Mwah! And Merry Christmas to you both. The place is a wonderland, an absolute wonderland!" Before either woman could draw breath for a question, he extended his arm toward the couple on the steps behind him, declaring, "Allow me to introduce Frieda and Geoffry Stein, our guests from the Hummingbird House. I'm sure you've heard me speak of them. Their stay with us has been an absolute delight."

The only guests Cici had heard Paul or Derrick mention over the past week were the ones they called "the couple from hell" so the lie was fairly transparent, as was the desperation in Paul's eyes as he told it. "The most dreadful thing," Paul went on quickly, "a pipe broke in the basement, completely flooded out the furnace, and of course no one can come out to look at it until after Christmas. The entire lodge is like a meat locker! A very damp meat locker at that. And wouldn't you know the Steins' flight home was canceled, although they were able to get on another one—which was a miracle itself on Christmas Eve!—but it doesn't leave until midnight. And of course, we couldn't have them freezing at the Hummingbird House, so we were so hoping you'd show mercy on us and…"

"Oh, for heaven's sake." Bridget pushed past him impatiently, a hand extended to the couple on the steps, her smile warm. "Come in, come in out of the cold. I'm Bridget and this is my friend Cici. Welcome to Ladybug Farm."

Cici widened her eyes at Paul with an explicit message of indignation and reprimand, and he pretended not to see. "Derrick is right behind us," he concluded cheerfully, "with a van full of Christmas gifts and booze. And his famous eggnog, of course! I told the shuttle driver he could pick the Steins up here at 9:00 tonight, if that's all right. Until then, we're all going to have just a marvelous time."

"Well, will you look at this!" exclaimed Frieda Stein, shrugging out of her coat. She was a short woman in her mid to late sixties whose blondish curls clung to her scalp when she pulled off her knit hat. She clasped her hands to her plump cheeks and looked around in delight. "Why, it's like a fairy tale! Isn't it like a fairy tale, Geof? Remember that castle in Vienna we visited that year? It wasn't nearly as darling as this. But it did have a skating rink. Oh, my goodness! Are these ornaments handmade?"

She went over to the Christmas tree, still chatting —although to whom, no one could guess. Bridget followed her, looking bemused.

The man, Geoffery, was heavy jowled and heavy browed, which gave him the look of a man constantly scowling. Later, they would all learn it wasn't just a look. He shrugged out of his overcoat and thrust it at Cici without glancing at her. "Looks like a Hallmark movie threw up in here," he muttered, and made his way toward the fireplace, hands outstretched for warmth.

"He'll be fine," Paul assured Cici sotto-voce. "He's been slamming back Irish coffees all morning. Put a whiskey in his hand and you won't hear another peep out of him. His wife, on the other hand, takes some getting used to."

Cici hung the stranger's coat on the hall tree while his wife went on brightly, "… and then I said to her, this can't possibly be prince's bedroom because the royal colors are blue and gold, and this room is red and white, but do you know what? It was! I was completely wrong. But you know the thing about…"

Cici whispered, "You could have given me some notice! It's not as though we don't have anything going on around here, you know!"

"I texted you," Paul insisted defensively.

She glared at him. "And you know I can only receive texts when the moon is full and the wind is out of the north."

"I wonder why that is," he mused. "I can send a text perfectly well from only six miles away, but you never get it."

"It's not the router," Kevin announced, coming out of the office. "The internet is down again. Hey, Paul, I didn't think you guys were coming over until tomorrow." He noticed the two strangers with a curious look and lowered his voice as he reached Cici. "Who, um…?"

Paul started to explain but Cici cut him off with, "It's a long story." To Paul, she said, "Of course you're welcome to wait here, I just wish…"

"They'll be no trouble, I promise," Paul put in, somewhat plaintively. "And it's only for a few hours."

The door opened on another gust of snowy air and Derrick edged his way in, laden down by two enormous suitcases. "Which guest room should I take our luggage to?" he inquired brightly.

~*~

It was hard to be annoyed with someone who

not only brought two cases of liquor and so many exquisitely wrapped Christmas presents that furniture had to be moved in order to fit them all under the tree but who then cheerfully volunteered to help out in the kitchen and was actually good at it. If there was one thing at which Paul and Derrick excelled, it was endearing themselves to the ladies of Ladybug Farm. Even Ida Mae, who didn't like anyone, managed to shift to an attitude of grudging tolerance when the gentlemen from the Hummingbird House visited.

Bridget left Geoffry Stein in a wing chair in front of the fireplace with a glass of whiskey in his hand, listening to a podcast through his earbuds and glaring at absolutely nothing, while his wife directed her nonstop monologue at Lori. She felt a little guilty for leaving Lori alone, but it really was every woman for herself.

Bridget slipped into the kitchen and the last strains of Frieda's remarks could be heard: "Of course, we're Jewish, so we don't really celebrate, but I do love all the lights and decorations, don't you? Where did you go to school, dear? Did you like it? What was your major? I remember when I was your age…"

Bridget closed the kitchen door and leaned against it, her eyes reflecting the relief of someone who had narrowly escaped a stampede of wild cattle. "My goodness," she breathed, "She is a chatty one, isn't she?"

The kitchen had become the refuge of everyone

who had tried to make conversation with their houseguests—except for Ida Mae, of course, who barely even acknowledged their arrival but remained standing over the double boiler, beating corn syrup and egg whites with a portable electric mixer. Paul, Derrick, and Cici had an assembly line going as they wrapped dishes for tomorrow's party and loaded them into market bags. Kevin carried the bags from the kitchen to his SUV for transportation to the Tasting Table's refrigerator at the bottom of the hill. The mixer droned in the background.

"Who did you leave as hostage?" Cici asked, glancing up from the cookies she was stacking into airtight containers.

"Lori," Bridget replied apologetically. "I thought…"

"She was too slow to get away," provided Cici with only a touch of sarcasm. "Good thinking."

Bridget gave her a look of reprimand. "I *thought*," she corrected archly, "Lori needed a chance to put her feet up."

"Ladies, ladies," admonished Paul, "the Christmas spirit, remember?"

"Easy for you to say," Cici grumbled. "You're not trying to get ready to give a party for fifty people tomorrow while dealing with unexpected overnight guests…"

"And icy roads," put in Bridget, frowning at the snow that drifted down in relentless white sheets outside the kitchen window.

"Oh, for heaven's sake, Bridget," Cici returned

impatiently, "the roads are fine. The weather report didn't say anything about ice."

"My, my," murmured Derrick. "We are a little testy today, aren't we?"

Cici gave him one of her killer scowls, but before she could say anything Lori came through the swinging door, her eyes on her phone, lumbering with the excess weight and cupping her belly with one hand while scrolling through her phone with the other. Oddly enough, the voice of Frieda Stein could still be heard chattering away.

"It's Aunt Lindsay's fault," Lori said. "And why is Tik-Tok down?"

"Tik-Tok isn't down," Cici reported, "our server is."

"Gee, what a surprise." Scowling, Lori put away her phone and sank heavily to a chair, wincing as she did so. "I have a new promotion for the winery launching today and I wanted to see how it's doing. And what's the story on those strange people in the parlor, anyway?" She could see a reprimand coming from her mother and waved it away pre-emptively. "They're fine. She's knitting something, and he just sat there staring at me like he'd never seen a pregnant woman before. It was creepy. I said I had to go to the bathroom, which I did, but I doubt anyone noticed me leave. So who are they?"

Cici looked meaningfully at Paul and Derrick. "Something we'd all like to know."

"Truthfully," replied Derrick, carefully tucking one last cookie into a container before snapping on the lid, "we don't know that much about them ourselves. They were a last-minute reservation…"

"Only one night," supplied Paul. "And since we were preparing to close for the holiday anyway…"

"We happened to have the vacant room," finished Derrick.

"Of course, we've been in *such* a frenzy preparing for New Year's Eve," Paul added, referring to the annual Hummingbird House New Year's Eve gala that drew attendees from far and wide.

"I'm afraid we didn't make our usual effort to get to know our guests," Derrick said apologetically, "and it is rather a challenge to have a conversation with Mrs. Stein…"

"Not to mention the fact that he never takes his earbuds out, not even at dinner." Paul sounded righteously miffed. Gracious living was one of the hallmarks of the Hummingbird House, and guests were expected to act appropriately.

"But," continued Derrick, "as far as I can tell, they're one of those retired couples who live on cruise ships, traveling around the world. They had a break between cruises and spent the last week skiing in West Virginia before they leave to catch the next ship in Miami the day after tomorrow."

"Oh, what fun," exclaimed Bridget. "Do you know, I hear it's actually cheaper for most seniors to live on a cruise ship than to keep a house?"

"I think it's a ridiculous way to live," replied Cici. She took a broom and dustpan from the closet and started sweeping up the crumbs around the table.

"Move your feet." She nudged Bridget's sneaker with the broom.

Bridget danced her feet out of the way, declaring irritably, "For heaven's sake, Cici, we're working here!"

"What do you think I'm doing, playing bridge?" Cici gave a particularly enthusiastic sweep of the broom just as Bridget reached to move half a tray of decorated cookies from the table to the countertop. On the backswing, the broom handle caught Bridget's elbow and the cookies went flying.

Bridget cried, "Now look what you did!"

Cici returned, "Me? I told you to move!"

Lori exclaimed, "Mom! My cookies!"

Derrick and Paul rushed to help Bridget scoop up the broken cookies from the floor. Lori lumbered to her feet but by the time she reached the scene of the disaster, Cici was already sweeping the last of the cookie shards into the dustpan. Ida Mae barely glanced around. Except for the whine of the portable mixer, the silence in the room was as taut as an electric wire.

"Do you know," Paul ventured after a moment, dusting off his hands, "I do believe Lori is right. Lindsay was definitely a calming influence on you two."

Ida Mae gave a derisive snort over the sound of the mixer. It was amazing what the old woman could hear when she wanted to. "Got nothing to do with it," she declared. "Two women's always gonna snipe at each other. Three's a balance."

"Like a three-legged stool," agreed Derrick, looking pleased with his metaphor. "That makes perfect sense."

Kevin said, "I am so not getting involved with this." He looped three bags filled with covered containers over each arm. "I'll be back for more."

"Be careful on the ice," Bridget called after him.

"There is no ice," Cici said tightly. She added deliberately to Ida Mae, "And we're not sniping."

Kevin opened the door on a gust of cold air and left quickly.

Cici looked uncomfortable as she glanced at Bridget, "I'm sorry if I was snarky."

Bridget smiled sheepishly. "I'm sorry I yelled at you about the cookies."

Cici hooked her foot around the rung of a chair and pulled it back from the table, then sat down heavily, resting her chin on her palm. "What in the world were we thinking, Bridge? Trying to do this all by ourselves. The decorating, the Christmas party for fifty people, Noah's homecoming dinner, all in the middle of our busiest shipping season for the winery and with twin grandbabies on the way. What are we trying to prove, anyway? It's stupid."

Bridget sighed, "I don't know. I just, you know, wanted it to be like the old days. But I think they're right about Lindsay." She gestured helplessly around the room, "This is our first Christmas without her in what? Twenty years? Maybe we're all trying too hard to make everything festive when nothing is really very festive at all."

"She's right." Lori lowered herself carefully to a kitchen chair, grunting with the effort. "It's like… what are we celebrating, anyway? I never thought anything could break up the ladies of Ladybug Farm, but…" She shrugged. "Nothing feels right anymore, does it?"

"What in the world are you people jabbering about?" Ida Mae turned off the mixer and ejected the paddles into the sink with a forceful clatter. "We're celebratin' the birth of baby Jesus, that's what. We've been doing it long before Red came along and we'll be doing it long after, so just shut your whining and give me some room over there. I got a cake to frost."

"Red" was Ida Mae's nickname for the auburn-haired Lindsay, and hearing it again drew a rueful smile from Bridget. She moved quickly to help Cici clear a space on the table amidst the plastic wrap, trays of food, and empty containers. "Sorry, Ida Mae," she said. "I guess it's too easy to forget the meaning of the season when we're caught up in all this chaos. Maybe we're getting too old for these parties."

Ida Mae grunted in agreement as she shuffled over to the worktable with the bowl of boiled icing held carefully between her hands. "Not gonna argue with you there."

Paul took the bowl of frosting from Ida Mae and set it on the table while Derrick went to the refrigerator to retrieve the cake. "Anyway, sweetie," Paul told Lori, "there's plenty to celebrate, what with little Paulette and Derrick coming along…"

"Sydney and Sherry," corrected Bridget.

"Piper and Portman," corrected Lori.

Cici made a face and shook her head decisively. Paul ignored them both and put an arm around Lori's shoulders, squeezing gently. "And don't forget you're a part of Ladybug Farm, now. Maybe the most important part. So the ladies of Ladybug Farm are still safely intact. "

Lori smiled at him gratefully, and then grew thoughtful. "You know, that's true. The place couldn't run without me. So I guess change can be a good thing. Sometimes." She sighed and stroked the mountain of her abdomen in an absent, self-soothing way. "But if I had one wish this Christmas —I mean aside from the babies being healthy, of course—it would be to have Aunt Lindsay back."

Cici gave her daughter a tolerant smile and Bridget patted her affectionately atop her head. "Us, too, sweetheart," she said.

Paul added quietly, "Us, four."

Derrick set the towering three-layer cake on the table. "Ida Mae, is this a Lane cake?" There was a note of awe in his tone. "I thought you said it was too much trouble, and you were never making it again."

Ida Mae scraped a chair along the stone floor as she pulled it away from the table and sat down heavily. "A person can change her mind, can't she? And this is a special occasion."

Paul and Derrick looked both delighted and puzzled, and Cici shrugged in answer to their unasked question. "We told her Noah doesn't like

Lane cake."

Ida Mae dipped a spatula into the fluffy white frosting. "I ain't making it for him."

Derrick's face cleared with understanding, "Ah," he said, nodding. "A tribute to Lindsay."

"So she'll be here in spirit," added Paul approvingly.

"The girl ain't dead," snapped Ida Mae, scooping up another dollop of frosting. "Stop talking like she is."

Paul sighed and pulled out a chair across from Ida Mae. "She's right," he said, "Lindsay is a grown woman and perfectly capable of making her own decisions, I just wish…"

"She'd made a different one," agreed Cici sadly. "Don't we all?" With a resigned breath, she squared her shoulders and started stacking sausage balls into a container.

"I don't suppose you've heard from her?" Derrick said hopefully.

"A couple of weeks ago," Bridget answered. "She wouldn't even talk about coming home, not even for a few days." She tore off a strip of plastic wrap but paused before placing it over the tray of freshly made deviled eggs, her expression morose. "We sent her Christmas presents to her sister in Florida, but that was before we knew Noah was coming here first. I guess he'll drive down to see her before New Year's, so we could have saved the postage on the presents."

"She did say she'd try to call tomorrow," added

Cici, forcing a note of cheerfulness into her voice. "That'll be nice."

"I don't get it," Lori said. "Aunt Lindsay doesn't even like her sister that much. Why would she want to go live with her when we're her family?"

Bridget looked at her daughter-in-law with the compassion of one who has seen heartbreak and knows what lies ahead, even while hoping desperately the younger woman will never understand the truth of it. She said, "I don't think it's that she doesn't want to be with us. It's just that..." She paused, searching for words. "I think it might be too painful to be here."

"But this is her home," Lori objected.

Cici placed a comforting hand on Lori's shoulder. "Honey, when something bad happens, it's like every single thing you see can cause you to relive that moment, that horrible loss. Dominic passed away here. He and Lindsay were so happy here, they had so many plans, and his stroke was so sudden, so unexpected... naturally being here just reminds her of the worst day of her life."

"It's been months, Mom," Lori said quietly. "The babies will be here soon. I want them to know her. Do you think she'll ever come home?"

Bridget and Cici exchanged a look that was filled with helplessness and sorrow. Paul covered Derrick's hand with his own, and Cici said simply, "I don't know."

There was a sudden sharp shrilling from the far wall of the kitchen, and everyone started. Derrick looked around in mild alarm. "Is that… a *phone*?"

Cici gave him a derisive look. "It's called a landline, Derrick. It's the only thing that works around here." She went to answer it.

"Maybe it's her," Lori said hopefully, struggling once again to get to her feet. "Maybe it's Aunt Lindsay, calling early."

But it wasn't Lindsay.

Three

Waiting for Christmas

"Noah!" Cici shouted into the phone, "Noah, is that you? Can you hear me?"

A burst of static came back at her as everyone gathered around, leaning close to try to hear the voice on the other end. Finally, it came. "Sorry!" Noah said. He sounded as though he was in a tunnel. "Been trying to call.... Phone's almost dead..." He said something about a lost charger, and then, "Listen..." His voice faded. "Very important. Wanted... surprise, but..." Static, static. "Missed connection so..."

"What?" Cici demanded. "Noah, you're breaking up, Where are you? Is your flight late? Do you need a ride from the airport?"

"We can go," Paul said, trying to take the telephone receiver from her. "Let me talk to him."

"No," Noah was saying when Cici retrieved the receiver again. "...fine. Just make sure that..." Again his voice faded into silence.

Cici looked helplessly at the other four. "But you'll be here, right? We're so excited about seeing you…"

Bridget tried for the phone, and when Cici shrugged away, holding the receiver to her ear like a prize jewel, Bridget called, "I'm making all your favorites, Noah! Spaghetti and chocolate pie and…"

Noah's voice came choppily again in Cici's ear. "On my way, but…" Static, silence. Then, "I know it's not… okay, right? You're not mad are you?"

"Mad? Why would I be mad? Noah…"

"Should have told you before but…." Nothing. "Just tell…"

"Tell what?" cried Cici, frustrated. "Tell who?"

Static. "Breaking up… But you've got this, right?" More static. "…can count on you."

"Yes, of course, whatever you need," Cici promised recklessly. "But, Noah, I didn't exactly hear what you said, so…Noah?" Silence. "Noah, are you there?" Not even static this time. "Hello?"

Three short beeps indicated the dropped call.

Cici replaced the receiver and looked around uncertainly at the anxious faces awaiting her.

"Well?" demanded Lori. "Is he on his way?"

"Everything's all right, isn't it?" Bridget said. "He didn't cancel, did he? After everything else, I don't think I could stand it if…"

"What did he say?" Paul put in. "We're happy to get in the SUV and…"

Cici held up a hand and shook her head helplessly. "I could barely hear him," she admitted. "So the answer is… I don't know. We'll just have to wait and see."

The disappointment was almost palpable as everyone turned away.

Ida Mae said testily, "You gonna let your company sit in there all by their lonesome? Fine way to show your Christmas hospitality, if you ask me." She made a careful divot in the frosted cake with her offset spatula, turned the cake half a degree, and repeated the gesture.

"Oh, dear," said Bridget, "I said I was going to bring them a pot of hot chocolate, I suppose I'd better make it." She went to the stove and took a pot from the overhead rack. "Lori, would you…?"

"My back hurts," Lori protested. "Anyway, I've got Christmas presents to wrap. I'll be in the office."

"The office is not a gift-wrapping station," Cici said, for perhaps the tenth time this week. "You left a mess all over the desk. Anyway, if your back hurts, you should lie down. We'll call you for dinner."

Lori gave her a disparaging look. "Are you kidding? Lying down is the *worst* thing you can do when you're carrying fifty-two extra pounds around your middle. That's why I haven't slept in two days. Honestly, Mom, don't you know *anything* about being pregnant?"

Cici sucked in a breath to reply, but let it out slowly and silently. She curled her fingers into her palms and forced a stiff smile.

Derrick said quickly, "I'll go see if our guests need anything." He started toward the door and then looked back apologetically. "Maybe a plate of canapes?"

Cici waved a careless hand. "Help yourself."

Derrick began to arrange cheese puffs and sausage balls on a plate and Bridget started heating milk and cocoa powder on the stove. Cici looked out the window. "The snow's letting up," she remarked.

"Thank goodness," Bridget said. Her expression was wistful as she stirred sugar into the cocoa mixture. "Remember that Christmas that we spent all day waiting for Noah to come home?"

"Hottest Christmas on record," Paul said with a shake of his head. "How could we forget?"

Cici suppressed a shudder. "He was out on that motorcycle by himself and Lindsay was sure something happened to him. Turns out, she was right."

"We spent the whole day sitting on the porch, telling stories about our favorite Christmas," Bridget added. "And in the end…"

"Everything turned out just fine," supplied Derrick, adding a sprig of parsley to his canape plate and stepping back to admire his work.

"It usually does," agreed Cici, smiling at Bridget.

After a moment, Bridget smiled back. "Yeah," she agreed, "It usually does."

Ida Mae finished the last decorative scallop of icing on the cake and regarded it with satisfaction. "Done," she declared, and carefully placed the glass dome over the cake plate.

"Ida Mae, it's beautiful," Paul said sincerely. "It will be the centerpiece of the dessert table."

She scowled at him. "I didn't make it to set it out

for all them heathens," she said. "This is my special homecoming cake. Now." She used both hands to push up from the table. "Somebody hand me my cane. I got to get upstairs and put fresh sheets on the bed in the spare room."

"Oh, don't bother," Derrick said quickly, taking her elbow to steady her on her feet. "We already made up our room and the Steins aren't staying the night."

"And Noah's room has been ready for a week," added Bridget.

"I ain't doing it for them," Ida Mae returned sourly and held out her hand, palm up, for her cane.

Cici hurried to bring her cane. "Do you need any help?" she offered, knowing what the answer would be.

Ida Mae grunted a disdainful reply and left the room, cane clacking.

Cici waited until she was out of sight to say, half whispering, "Poor thing. I don't think she understands that Lindsay isn't going to be here."

Derrick looked after her sympathetically, and Bridget said, "Still, you've got to admire her gumption. A hundred and two years old, and still going up and down those stairs like a teenager."

Paul's eyebrows shot up in surprise. "Is that how old she is?"

"Nobody knows how old she is," replied Cici. "It's one of those cosmic mysteries, like how many angels can dance on the head of a pin. Take the cake into the butler's pantry, will you?"

The back door opened as Paul returned from the pantry and Derrick, with a bottle of whiskey in one hand and the plate of canapes in the other, left to attend to the Steins.

"The snow's stopped," Kevin announced, stamping the remnants of snow off his boots, "so I swept off the steps while I was out there. It's going to be Lori's favorite kind of Christmas—snow on the ground, none in the air." He glanced around, "Where is she?"

"Wrapping presents," Cici said. "Or so she said. I think she's probably trying to get the internet working again."

"Well, a car just pulled into the driveway," Kevin replied. "It looked like it might be a ride-share. Could Noah have gotten in early?"

"*That's* why he called!" he exclaimed Cici delightedly. "To tell us he was on his way!"

Bridget clapped her hands together happily and jerked at the ties of her apron. "Oh, thank goodness! Now everything is going to be okay!" She smoothed down her hair with her fingers, paused to turn the burner off under the hot chocolate, and practically skipped through the swinging doors to the main room.

Cici followed, calling, "Lori! Noah's here!"

But it wasn't Noah.

Four

The Christmas Visitor

They all were gathered at the big front window when the white sedan with the Uber sticker in the window pulled up. In the background, Frieda Stein exclaimed, "Oh, my, more guests! This place is busier than the B&B, isn't it, Geof? But then it is the holidays!"

The passenger side rear door of the car opened and a figure got out. Just as everyone was about to flood the front porch to welcome their missing family member, they stopped. The person who got out of the car wasn't Noah. Instead, it was a young woman in a red wool coat and a green stocking hat with a multi-colored knit scarf wrapped around her neck. She hoisted a tapestry bag over her shoulder and stood looking up at the house for a moment with both trepidation and expectation in her eyes. The Uber pulled away and she squared her shoulders, then started determinedly up the steps.

The others looked at one another in puzzlement, and Cici went to the door. She opened it just as the young woman lifted her hand to knock.

"Hello," Cici said, smiling cautiously and wishing

the girl had not sent her car away. "Can I help you?"

The young woman smiled broadly. She was a beauty in her early twenties with creamy skin, big brown eyes, and a shiny black ponytail draped over one shoulder. "Hello," she replied in oddly accented, carefully enunciated English. "I am so pleased to meet you."

"Oh," replied Cici, at a complete loss.

Lori edged her way forward. "Who is it?"

The young woman's smile faded into dismay, and then cleared hopefully as she fumbled in her pocket and brought out her phone. She scrolled a couple of screens and then held up the phone to Cici. On the screen was clearly printed: Ladybug Farm, 113 Highway 17 North, Blue Valley, Virginia.

"Oh," said Cici again, her confusion deepening. "I mean, yes. Yes, that's right. That's us."

"Cici!" hissed Bridget behind her. "Don't keep her standing in the cold!"

The young lady was busily typing something into her phone and didn't notice when Cici stepped back and opened the door wider. Bridget pushed forward with a welcoming, "Won't you come in?" When she received no reply, she touched the girl's arm, gesturing her inside.

The girl tapped her screen a few more times in what appeared to be growing frustration. Then, with a helpless look, she stepped inside.

Paul whispered, "Do you think she's deaf?"

Derrick gave him a scathing look and whispered back, "The word is non-hearing."

"Hello, my dear," Paul said loudly, and Derrick rolled his eyes. "Can you hear me?"

The girl looked at him with a tenuous smile, "Hello," she repeated. "I am so pleased to meet you."

"What is she doing with our address on her phone?" Cici wondered out loud.

"Well, apparently she's where she's supposed to be," Bridget said with a bewildered frown.

Once again the girl held up a finger for patience and started typing into her phone.

Kevin said, "I don't think she speaks English."

Lori came around to peer over the newcomer's shoulder. "I think you're right. She's typing into Google translator." She looked up at Kevin. "Which doesn't work without..."

"The internet," Kevin finished for her grimly.

Their visitor had apparently just come to the same realization because she looked up from her phone with a desperate look in her eyes and let forth a stream of passionate declarations that were completely incomprehensible to anyone besides herself.

"Oh, my goodness," Bridget said softly, resting a hand on her throat.

Paul frowned, "What language is that? Do you recognize it, Derrick?"

Cici smiled apologetically at the girl and opened her hands in a shrug. "I'm sorry. We don't understand."

Kevin came over to her and, through smiles and gestures, persuaded her to let him look at her phone.

After a brief moment he returned it to her with a grateful smile and told the others, "You got me. Could be Greek, could be Cyrillic…"

"Chinese?" suggested Lori.

He shook his head. "I don't think so, Anyway, she doesn't look Asian, does she?"

The girl started speaking again, using broad gestures and increasingly desperate facial expressions. When she finished, all they could do was look at her in mute apology.

Ida Mae stood at the back of the group, arms crossed, a ferocious frown on her face. "Russian," she declared fiercely. "She's a damn Russian spy."

"Oh, for heaven's sake, Ida Mae," Bridget replied impatiently, "What would a Russian spy want from us? Your fruitcake recipe?"

"They're all over the inter-web," Ida Mae insisted, still scowling. "I listen to the news, I hear things. Taking over this country, that's what they're doing."

"The question remains," said Kevin, "what's she doing here?"

The girl started talking again in her incomprehensible language, her expression and intonation fluctuating from hope to despair to question to assertation and, finally, back to despair.

Cici said, "Well, we can't just leave her standing in the hall. Someone gave her our address."

"Oh, my goodness," Bridget said softly, Her eyes lit with excitement. "Oh, my goodness, I think I know who!" She turned to Cici. "Reverand Holland, remember? He said he had a mission family visiting for Christmas and wanted to know if he could bring them to the Christmas party and I said, of course! This has got to be one of them!"

Cici said cautiously, "I'm not sure I was in on that conversation."

"She just got the date wrong, that's all," Bridget insisted. She turned happily to the stranger and said, "Reverand Holland? Yes?"

The girl, looking as confused and disoriented as ever, just smiled weakly.

Bridget squeezed her arm. "I'll just go call him and let him know she's here. We'll have this all worked out in no time. Meantime, Kevin, take her bag and her coat. Let's get her comfortable in front of the fire. She must be exhausted! And then to end up at the wrong house. You just make yourself at home, honey," she told the stranger, giving her arm another reassuring squeeze. "We're going to get you where you belong. I'll be right back."

Lori looked skeptically at her mother as Bridget hurried back to the kitchen to make the phone call. "Um, I don't think…"

"Doesn't matter," said Cici firmly. "We don't turn anybody away at Christmas."

She turned to the girl with an encouraging smile. "I'm Cici," she said. "Welcome."

A look of overwhelming relief flooded the girl's face and she pressed both hands to her chest. "Nora," she said.

"Delighted to meet you, Nora," Cici replied. She

gestured toward the parlor as Kevin gently relieved her of her bag and Paul gracefully helped her out of her coat, hat, and scarf. "Come sit down."

"No," she said, once again looking distressed as she fixed her gaze on Cici. "*Nora.*"

Cici forcefully deepened her smile. "Okay," she said. "This is Lori, and Kevin, and Paul, and Derrick, and Ida Mae." She touched each person as she said the name, then gently placed a hand on the girl's shoulder and guided her toward the fireplace. "I know it's a lot, but we're friendly, I promise. And these people are..."

"Frieda Stein," said Freida. She put aside her needlework and came forward with her hand extended. "Aren't you a pretty little thing? This is my husband Geoff." She poked her husband on the shoulder with her finger and he grunted acknowledgement. "We don't live here," she went on cheerily. "Just wayward travelers, like you. Come sit by me, dear, We'll have a chat."

"Um, she doesn't speak English," Cici started to explain, but Nora interrupted her hopefully.

"*Sprechen Sie Deutsch*?"

"German!" exclaimed Lori excitedly, "I recognize that. She's German!"

Nora reacted to Lori's enthusiasm by pressing her hands together in delight, "*Ja, ja! Deutsch! Ja!*"

"Which isn't very helpful at all," Kevin pointed out, "unless someone else here speaks German." He looked around the room questioningly.

"Oh, my," admitted Frieda. "I'm afraid not. Geoff

speaks a little Latin, though." She bent to remove one of her husband's earbuds and spoke loudly to him. "Don't you speak Latin, dear?"

"Doesn't matter," he replied gruffly. "The girl is Russian." He replaced the earbud and held out his whiskey glass for a refill. Derrick was quick to oblige.

Ida Mae snorted in satisfaction and planted herself in the rocking chair by the window where she could keep a wary eye on the group, hands crossed atop her cane as though readying herself to use it as a weapon on a moment's notice.

"You know," Lori observed, lowering her voice a little to keep her words private from the newcomer, "there are lots of translation apps that don't use the internet. I wonder why she didn't download one of those?"

Kevin shrugged. "Most civilized countries actually have access to the internet. She probably didn't think she'd need it."

Cici gave him a mildly insulted look and insisted, "We're civilized. Just," she admitted, "maybe not today so much."

Frieda, meantime, had guided Nora to the flowered loveseat beside the fireplace and gestured her to be seated. She sat down beside her and inquired solicitously, "Do you speak any English at all, dear?"

"Um," replied Nora, looking uncomfortable. "Ah... English."

Everyone gathered close, listening eagerly.

Nora wrinkled her forehead and said, very

carefully, "Take me... to the hotel." She looked around uncertainly for approval, then added, "Where is the public..." She pronounced it *pooblik.* "Rester... resting...room."

"The bathroom?" supplied Cici helpfully, "It's just down the..."

"I don't think she really wants the bathroom, Mom," Lori said impatiently. "She just learned a bunch of phrases out of one of those travel books."

"Like no one we know has ever done *that,*" remarked Kevin with a slight upward roll of his eyes. "Remember how you were when you first got to Italy?"

Frieda prompted, "Do you know any other English at all, dear?"

At that moment Bridget came in, carrying a tray of cookies, hot chocolate, and mugs. Paul quickly went to help her with it. "Well," Bridget announced, doing her best to sound upbeat, "there was no answer at Reverand Holland's but I left a voice mail. Of course, the pastor has Christmas Eve services so it may be a while before he gets back to us. I'm sure this will all get straightened out as soon as he does, though. Meanwhile..." She poured chocolate from the pot into a mug and offered it to Nora with a big smile. "Let's all just settle back and get acquainted, shall we?"

Nora took the chocolate with a weak smile of gratitude that faded too soon. "I am," she said unhappily, dropping her eyes to her mug, "so pleased to meet you."

~*~

For the next endless hour, they waited awkwardly, if not in silence, sipping cocoa and eating far too many cookies. The phone did not ring; Noah did not arrive. It turned out Frieda's sewing project was not knitting, but tatting, and when Cici made the mistake of admitting she did not know what that was, she was treated to a lecture on the subject that showed no sign of letting up. When Nora—whether from pity or boredom—actually appeared interested, Frieda shared the project with her and, of all the amazing things, Nora seemed to be familiar with the process. Everyone relaxed a little to see two of their guests, at least, gainfully occupied.

Bridget looked nervously at the clock. "Maybe I should call the church office," she said.

"It's Christmas Eve," Derrick pointed out. "I doubt anyone will be working."

She sighed and sat back in her chair. "You're probably right."

Kevin returned from the kitchen and announced, "I tried calling Noah again. Voicemail. If his phone was dying when he talked to you, Aunt Cici, it's got to be completely dead by now."

"His flight should have landed two hours ago," Cici said. She couldn't help sounding worried. "It's getting dark outside."

Kevin said, "He's a..."

"Great big strong Marine," Bridget supplied,

"completely capable of driving in the dark, I know."

Lori bit down on another cookie. "Who travels without a phone charger anyway?"

"You do." Kevin kissed her hair and added another log to the fire. "Every time we go anywhere."

She shot him a dark look but, surprisingly, let it go. Instead, she took another bite of her cookie. "Do you know what this reminds me of?" she said.

Bridget and Cici both looked around the room in muted perplexity. The deeply disgruntled man who blocked out the world with earbuds and whiskey; the two strangers—one who couldn't stop talking and one who couldn't talk at all— with their heads bent over a common bit of lacework; Ida Mae, scowling over them all from her rocking chair like a soldier on sentry duty. There was nothing about the scene that was in any way reminiscent of anything… or at least, not anything pleasant.

When no one answered her, Lori insisted, "That story. You know, the one Nana used to tell every Christmas about the family that was waiting for this distinguished guest to show up for Christmas Eve— the mayor or president or somebody…"

"Oh, I know that one!" exclaimed Freida.

Paul gave her a puzzled look. "I thought you were Jewish."

"Oh, we are," she assured him airily. "More or less. But I do love a good holiday story."

"Anyway," Lori went on, "they were all excited, you know, killed the fatted calf, put out the good china, polished up the silver, wrapped up expensive presents, getting everything all ready for the mayor…"

"It was a prophet." Ida Mae spoke up gruffly. "It was back in Bible days and they was waiting for the prophet."

"That's what they called all important men back in those times," Derrick explained helpfully to Freida.

"Right," said Lori. "Whatever. So they're all dressed up, waiting for their Christmas company, dinner's on the table, candles lit, everything just so, and who should come knocking at the door but an old dirty homeless guy…"

"Oh, I remember now," exclaimed Cici. "And the woman of the house felt so bad she invited him in and fed him dinner…"

"Which ruined her beautiful feast," said Lori. "And then…"

"There was a beggar woman, wasn't there?" put in Freida happily, "And she was freezing? Oh, this is a darling story. And then…"

"Right." Lori spoke over her firmly. "So they gave her the coat they'd bought as a present for the mayor —"

"Prophet," interrupted Ida Mae testily.

"…to impress him," Lori concluded.

"Big mistake," observed Paul.

"Just wait," Bridget told him, smiling. "I think you'll like this one."

"And then," went on Lori, "this is my favorite

—there was this mean-looking biker dude whose motorcycle broke down in front of their house and he asked if he could use the phone…"

"Weren't no phone back in them days," Ida Mae declared irritably. "You've got it all wrong."

Lori went on confidently, "So they let him in and he tracked mud all over the freshly cleaned carpet, and then he told how his little boy was sick in the hospital and there was no money for Christmas presents, and so they gave him their presents from under the tree…"

"Talk about gullible," murmured Paul, and Derrick shushed him loudly, eagerly turning his attention to Lori for the rest of the story.

"So anyway," Lori went on, "after all this, the house was a wreck, the food was all gone, the candles burned down, the Christmas presents taken…"

"Sounds like a typical Christmas at Ladybug Farm," Cici observed under her breath. Bridget suppressed a giggle, and Lori ignored both of them.

"The Christmas visitor finally gets there," she said. "The family was so embarrassed. They said, 'We were so foolish. We had such a beautiful Christmas all planned but we gave away the food and the presents and now we have nothing left for you.' But then the mayor—or whoever—just smiled and said, 'You've already given me everything I wanted. Because I was the homeless man, and I was the old woman, and I was the biker with the sick child.' Turns out, the person they'd been waiting for all the time was…"

"Moses!" exclaimed Freida.

Lori stared at her for a beat, expressionless, then turned back to the group. She finished, "Jesus. The man was Jesus."

"'Tweren't neither," argued Ida Mae. "It was an angel."

"The way I heard it," began Bridget.

"I'm telling you," insisted Ida Mae irately, "it was an angel."

"Well, I think you told it beautifully, sweetheart," Cici said firmly, forestalling the argument she could sense coming.

"So do I," agreed Kevin. He caught Lori's fingers and kissed them. "You're going to make a great mom."

Lori considered that for a moment and then nodded her head, "Yes, I am."

"Well, look at that," exclaimed Freida, holding up the piece of lace Nora had been working on. It was a beautifully executed square, in the center of which was an intricately woven star of David. "You finished it!"

Nora shrugged modestly and said, "*Et voila.*"

Lori seized on this eagerly, "French! That's what she is! *Parlez vous francais*?"

Nora's eyes lit up, "*Oui! Oui! Vous aussi? Merveilleux!*" She then launched forth into a string of rapid, effortless French exposition, complete with excited gestures, that left Lori wide-eyed and staring.

"Um," Lori said in a small voice, "I don't really *speak* French, per se." She looked around the room. "Anyone?"

One by one they shook their heads, and Derrick added helpfully, opening his hands wide, "*Désolé*."

Nora's excited expression fell away. Trying to cheer her, Bridget came over to examine the lacework. "It's beautiful," she told both women, smiling warmly. "A Christmas star!"

"Actually," began Freida, but Bridget did not give her a chance to finish.

Bridget held up the lace to Ida Mae. "Look, Ida Mae. Didn't you used to do tatting? Isn't this pretty?"

"Not bad," admitted Ida Mae grudgingly, "for a spy and a J—"

"I'm going to have a glass of wine." Cici cut Ida Mae off loudly, getting to her feet. "Can I pour one for anyone else?"

"I'll take one," Lori said. She held out one hand and with the other patted her belly. "This time next year."

Bridget rose, too. "And I suppose I'd better get supper started."

Both women tried to disguise their anxiety as they glanced toward the windows. The sky was fully dark now, the only illumination that of the Christmas lights dancing off the snow.

"It's a sweet story," Paul could be heard saying as the two women left the room. "But I don't understand why it reminded you of..."

Bridget said worriedly to Cici, "I know we should

wait for Noah, but it's getting late, and everyone is hungry."

"I don't see how they could be," offered Cici, "after all those cookies."

Bridget sighed, "Spaghetti and meatballs doesn't seem like much of a Christmas Eve dinner to offer company. I should probably slice up that ham."

"Jewish, remember?"

"Oh. Turkey, then."

Cici took down two glasses from the kitchen cabinet and filled each with wine. She handed one to Bridget. "I don't think it matters what you serve for dinner, Bridge," she said quietly. "Noah's not going to make it."

Bridget looked sadly over Cici's shoulder to the window fogged with snow and black with night. "I know."

They clinked glasses and drank.

Five

The Christmas Surprise

Cici leaned against the porch rail in the muted glow of the Christmas decorations, looking out over the blue-shadowed lawn. In the peculiar way of a fresh snowfall, the night did not seem particularly chill, and the reflected light from the snow cover chased away the darkness. The air was tinged with woodsmoke and cinnamon and fresh crisp evergreen. The occasional bleat of a restless sheep floated to her from the barn. Behind her, the electric candles in each wreathed window cast a golden circle of light upon the painted floorboards of the porch. The whole was a perfect portrait of holiday serenity, and every part of the scene only deepened her depression.

The door opened behind her, but Cici did not turn around. She took a sip of her wine and said, "Lindsay would paint this."

Bridget came to stand beside her, her own wine glass in hand. "Somebody should," she agreed. "It's beautiful." She sipped her wine. "I decided to slice up the turkey and serve it over croquettes of dressing with cranberry sauce and mashed potatoes. It'll be a while before the potatoes are done."

"Oh, Bridge, I should have helped you."

"That's okay. Kevin peeled the potatoes and Paul is setting the table and lighting a fire in the dining room. It's Christmas Eve, after all. People should have candles and good china and a real meal. I thought we'd slice the chocolate cake for dessert, and serve it with Derrick's eggnog."

Cici tried to smile but it came out rather melancholy. "This really is like Lori's story. We're going to give away all our food before the party even starts."

"Fat chance. Anyway, I feel sorry for that poor girl, Nora, all alone and lost on Christmas Eve in a country where she doesn't even speak the language. And the cruising couple, too. People should be at home for Christmas."

"Yes," said Cici, and she was surprised to hear her voice break a little at the end. "They should."

Bridget slipped her arm around Cici's waist. "Noah will be here, Cici. Maybe not tonight, but he'll call as soon as he can. He's a responsible young man."

"I know." Cici's voice was thick and she took a gulp of wine to clear it. "It's not that." She let out a heavy breath. "I'm just sad, Bridget. I'm so, so sad, and you were right before. Dressing up sadness in all this Christmas glitter just makes it all the more lonely. And pathetic."

"Oh, Cici." Bridget's voice was filled with gentle dismay. "Please don't cry. You never cry. I can't stand it when you cry."

Cici swiped the back of her hand across her eyes. "Everything changes so fast. Yesterday Noah was just a gangly teenager with an attitude and now he's a man with shoulders as broad as a house, out there fighting for our country. Our babies are having babies. Lindsay is… Lindsay has moved on, and I'm just thinking that maybe this time next year *we'll* be the ones living on a cruise ship because we have no place better to be."

Bridget pulled back, looking scandalized, "Cici!"

Cici shook her head sharply and blotted the dampness on her cheeks. "Lori and Kevin are too smart and too talented to stay here forever, you know that."

"They just built a house!"

"And the babies won't be babies forever. They'll need good schools and… Oh, my God!" Cici caught a wet gasp in her throat. "I'm going to be a *grandmother*!"

Bridget stared at her with big eyes. "Oh, my God," she repeated, as though understanding it for the first time. "So am I."

At her expression, Cici choked out a sound that was halfway between a laugh and a sob and wiped her running nose with the back of her hand. "We have so many memories here," she managed after a moment, unsteadily. "So many dreams that were born and mangled and reshaped and finally came to life… but we did it together. Dominic was such a big part of that. In a way…" She made a sweeping gesture with her wine glass to indicate the winery and the vineyard beyond, now shrouded in the mists of a winter night, "...he gave us all of this. And now he's gone." She took a sip of her wine and said, very lowly, "I miss him every single day."

Bridget covered Cici's hand on the rail with her own.

Cici drew a heavy breath and went on, "I understand how Lindsay feels, I really do. But the truth is, without her, we're not us anymore. And that's why I'm sad. Because I can't fix this. Nobody can. I just..." She swallowed hard, struggling to keep her voice even. She did not entirely succeed. "I just really don't want this to be our last Christmas memory here. Because it really sucks."

Bridget put down her wine glass and, without a word, folded her friend into her embrace. "Hey," she said, stepping away. "You know what they say. All will be well in the end. And if all is not well..."

"It's not the end," Cici finished. She blotted the last of the tears out of the corners of her eyes and forced a smile. "When did you get to be the wise one?"

Bridget shrugged modestly and picked up her wine glass again. "When needs must."

The door opened on a square of light and the background chatter of Freida Stein. "Hey, Aunt Bridget," Lori said, coming onto the porch. "Ida Mae said to tell you your potatoes are going to scorch if you don't watch them. But it's okay, I turned down the burner. Also, Pastor Holland returned your call. He said he didn't know anything about a foreign woman named Nora but he would try to find out what he could."

"Oh." Bridget's brow furrowed with confusion and disappointment. "That's too bad. I could have sworn…" But she let the thought drop and smiled at Lori. "Thanks, sweetheart," she said. "Where's your coat? You're going to catch your death."

Lori lifted her hair from the back of her neck and let it fall again. "I was burning up in there, sitting by the fire. I came out here to cool off."

Cici circumspectly patted the last traces of moisture from her face and rearranged her features into something resembling ease. She turned to her daughter. "You look flushed. Are you okay?"

"Burning up," Lori repeated, brushing away the hand her mother tried to place against her cheek. "You know what I don't understand," she said, resting her elbows on the railing between the two women, "is how that woman could come to America speaking three different languages, and not one of them is English. How dumb is that? Anyway, turns out she really did need the restroom, so I showed her where it was."

Cici gave her a dry look. "You want to talk about dumb? How about nine adults inside that house and none of them speaks anything *but* English. Who's really the dumb one?"

"I didn't mean dumb as in not smart," Lori explained impatiently. "Of course she's smart. But how about a little preparation? I mean, if she's depending on the internet to get to where she belongs she could be stuck here for days."

Neither woman could argue with that.

"Anyway," Lori said, "Kevin is calling the internet provider to find out when service will be restored."

"Good luck with that," remarked Bridget, "at 7:00 on Christmas Eve."

"That's what I said," Lori replied, pushing away from the railing. "But you know Kev. And speaking of which, I've got to finish wrapping his present. When's supper?"

"About half an hour," Bridget said, walking to the door with Lori.

Cici accompanied them. "What did you get him?" she asked Lori.

"It's the coolest thing." Lori's face lit up with pleasure at her own cleverness. "I found this place online where you can make a coffee table book out of your own photographs and stuff, so I sent in all the pictures we had of Italy—where we first met, our favorite trattoria, our apartment above the bakery, the flower market where we used to stop after every payday..." Her voice grew nostalgic and so did her smile as she cradled her babies with her arms. "It turned out great. And it's not only for Kev, but for the babies someday, too, so they'll know our whole story. And..."

The pleasure on her face abruptly disappeared and was replaced by something akin to horror as she gasped, "And I left it on the desk in the office where Kevin was going to make his phone call!"

She spun around to open the door and Cici cried,

"Lori don't run!"

The three of them made it to the office just as Nora was coming out of the bathroom across the hall and Kevin was hanging up the phone with an irritated frown on his face. The expression was quickly erased when he saw Nora, however, and he said, "Oh, hi. Are you lost?" He started to get up and added, gesturing broadly in the way people do when trying to make themselves understood by one who doesn't speak the language, "Sorry, I'll walk back with you."

Cici, with her long legs, was the first to reach the office and was relieved to see that Kevin didn't appear to have noticed his surprise Christmas gift lying in plain sight on the desk amidst a clutter of wrapping paper, ribbons and bows, twine and gift tags. To further distract him, she said loudly, "Kevin, there you are! Any luck with the internet?"

He was about to answer when Bridget and Lori arrived, both of them out of breath. Nora, apparently mistaking Kevin's gestures for an invitation, stepped inside the office and immediately spotted the book on the corner of the desk. She gave a small cry of delight and picked it up, exclaiming over the cover,

"*La Piazza Navona! La Fontana del Nettuno. Adoro questo posto!*" She looked at Kevin eagerly, "*Ci sei stato? È bellissimo, vero?*" She pressed the book to her chest, smiling dreamily, "*Così romantico!*"

Lori rushed forward, pushing past Cici and Bridget, "Excuse me, no, that's not..." She stopped short, staring at Nora. "Wait. You speak Italian?"

Kevin said at the same time, "You speak Italian?"

Nora looked uncertainly from one to the other of them. "*Italiano*?"

Kevin exclaimed, "I speak Italian! I mean, *Parlo Italiano!*" He thumped his chest excitedly, "*Parlo Italiano!*"

"Me, too!" cried Lori. "That is, kind of." But Nora and Kevin were already deep into a fast-flowing, gesticulating conversation that left Lori behind after the first sentence. She grabbed Cici's arm, laughing. "She speaks *Italian*!" Then, "Wait, My book."

Lori hurried forward and gently pried the book from Nora's hands. The other woman barely seemed to notice, so caught up was she in the delight of being able to communicate at last with someone who understood her. Lori grabbed a sheet of wrapping paper from the desk and wadded it around the gift, turning quickly to hide it from Kevin, who also didn't notice.

Bridget said, "Kevin, what's she saying?" Then to Lori, "What is she saying?"

Cici added, "Ask her who she is. What's she doing here?"

Kevin held up a hand for patience while Nora finished what she was saying, and then he asked her something in smooth, if rather urgent-sounding Italian.

Lori said, "Well, for one thing, her name is not Nora. It's Mariya. Or maybe Mary. At least that's the part I heard. And she's from some country I didn't understand. Does anyone see the tape?" She struggled to keep the wrapping paper from sliding off.

Kevin started laughing, "*Davvero? Seriamente?*" And then, while the other three women stared at him agape, he hugged the stranger. "*Benvenuta, Mariya, Benvenuto!*"

He turned around, holding the girl's arm, grinning. "Ladies, this is Mariya. She's a registered nurse and a newlywed from Crimea, lately of Germany. She came here with her husband, but they got separated when he missed a connection in New York. He's American so she didn't think her limited English would be a problem." His grin widened. "You will not believe who she's married to."

From behind them, a familiar male voice said, "Me."

"Noah!" Mariya sprang away from Kevin, pushed past the ladies hovering at the door, and threw herself into the arms of the tall man in a military service uniform. Her feet left the ground as Noah swept her up, laughing, kissing her, and the ladies just watched, paralyzed with astonishment.

Then Lori slapped her forehead, "Not Nora!" she exclaimed. "*Noah*! That's what she said. We just heard wrong!" She twisted around to look at Kevin, still trying to keep the package concealed. "Kevin, tape."

Her words jolted Cici and Bridget out of their shock and they surged forward, embracing first

Noah, then Mariya, then both of them.

"Noah, you're here!"

"We were so afraid you wouldn't make it! Oh, I'm so happy!"

"You're married? How can you be married? Why didn't you—"

"Noah, I can't believe it! Oh, it's so good to see you!"

Even as they bombarded him with questions and hugs, Noah held on to Mariya's hand, a grin splitting his face as he spoke to her. It took Bridget and Cici and moment to realize he was speaking in German.

Cici fell back, staring at him, "You speak German?"

He nodded and looked fondly at Mariya. "That's how we met, in German class. Mari had to get certified to work in Germany, and I was tired of living in a place where I couldn't even read the street signs once I left the base. Also..." He shrugged. "It was points toward a promotion. Anyway, that was a year ago. When I heard I was being transferred back to D.C. ..."

Bridget pressed her hands to her cheeks in delight. "You're being transferred!"

Kevin handed Lori the tape and draped an arm around her shoulders while she sloppily wrapped his Christmas present. "Told you that was the surprise," he said smugly.

"We got married at the embassy three days ago," Noah went on. "I'd rather have done it here, naturally, but with a military man marrying a foreign national it gets complicated and…"

"And *that*'s the surprise!" declared Cici.

"No," said another voice, just coming around the corner. "Actually, I am."

Six

A Christmas Homecoming

Lindsay came down the hall in snow boots, stocking hat, and puffer coat, her arms open wide. Bridget, Cici, and Lori rushed into her embrace, laughing and crying and all talking at once, almost knocking her down with their enthusiasm. Mariya and Noah hung back, smiling and talking softly to each other, and Kevin waited for a break in the reunion tears to wedge his way in between the ladies and draw Lindsay into an embrace.

"Merry Christmas, Aunt Lindsay," he said, smiling. "Man, it's good to see you! But let's go back in the parlor where there's a fire, what do you say?"

"Sounds good to me," said Lindsay. "My feet are frozen. Who is that woman in the parlor, anyway? She about talked my ear off before I could even get out of my coat!"

"Why are you so wet?" Bridget demanded, wrapping her arm around Lindsay's as they headed back to the main room. "It's not still snowing, is it?"

"It's been a hell of a trip," Noah said behind them. "We had to walk the last part of it. There's a big tree down across the road about a quarter mile back."

"We had to leave the luggage in the rental car," Lindsay said. "*And* the Christmas presents."

"We sent yours to Florida!" Bridget said, her face clouding with dismay.

"Anyway," said Cici, clasping Lindsay's free hand, "you're the only Christmas present we need. Gosh, we missed you!"

Lindsay smiled and squeezed her hand. "Same."

"But," Lori said hopefully, edging between the three women, "you got my baby registry link, didn't you?"

Lindsay laughed and drew Lori into a one-armed hug, "You, I missed most of all. And," she added, "you are the fattest pregnant woman I've ever seen."

Lori grinned at her. "I'm so glad you're back I'm not even going to punch you for that."

Paul and Derrick had been in the kitchen with Ida Mae when Lindsay and Noah arrived through the back door, so they had been the first to hear the details of the Christmas surprise. They waited now in the parlor with hot chocolate and shortbread cookies, full of their own self-importance and eager to supply salient details that Noah may have left out. Freida Stein was silent for once, listening in rapt attention as the story unfolded. Her husband sipped his whiskey and never once looked up from his scowling contemplation of the fire.

"I wanted you all there for the ceremony," Noah said, drawing Mariya down beside him on the flowered loveseat. "But getting you over there on such short notice..."

"Gracious, I don't even know where my passport is," Bridget said.

"Not to mention trying to get somebody to take care of the farm, and with Lori being too fat to fly..."

"Shut up," Lori said and tossed half a cookie at him.

Noah caught the cookie, grinning, and Paul supplied, "Actually, it was Lindsay who said you wouldn't want to leave Lori this close to term."

"But I knew exactly where my passport was," Lindsay said, "and of course, I'm going to be there when my only son gets married... even if 'there' is halfway around the world!"

"But you could have called us," Cici said. "You could have at least let us know."

Noah paused a minute to translate the conversation thus far to his wife and Bridget shook her head in wonder.

"I still can't believe he speaks German," she murmured.

Mariya said something back to Noah and he turned back to the ladies, "Mari says to tell you it's her fault. She's the one who said it would be foolish for you to spend the money on the trip when we were coming here in three days anyway. And that's what gave me the idea to surprise you." His expression turned wry as he sipped his cocoa. "A stupid idea, it turns out."

"It sure was," agreed Lori.

Derrick put in nobly, "I think it was a wonderful

idea. The best Christmas surprise ever.”

"Would have been,” said Noah, “if it had worked.”

"I don't understand how you got separated,” Cici said.

"Well,” began Paul, leaning forward to tell the tale. Cici silenced him with a look.

"Now, that was definitely Noah's fault,” Lindsay said, glancing sourly at Noah. “We had fifteen minutes to make it to the gate at La Guardia…”

"And you *know* what La Guardia is like on Christmas Eve,” put in Derrick with a shudder.

"I thought it would be a good idea to call you before we got onboard,” Noah said, “but my phone was almost dead and I couldn't find my charger…”

"He forgot to pack it,” Lindsay said with an indulgent eyeroll.

"But Mom *did* pack hers,” Noah put in pointedly, “right along with her phone in her checked luggage.”

Lindsay lifted one shoulder philosophically. “Which is now somewhere in Bosnia, by the way. The airline said they'd deliver it as soon as they found it.”

"So anyway, I saw a store that I thought might have a charger, so I sent Mom and Mariya ahead to the gate. They didn't have one, but a shop across the way looked like it might…”

"By this time the flight was boarding,” Lindsay said.

"These flights are never on time,” insisted Noah defensively.

"So I sent Mariya ahead and ran back to try to find

him," Lindsay said.

"Bad move," observed Lori.

"And that's how they both missed the flight," finished Derrick with a flourish, leaving both Noah and Lindsay to enjoy a sip of their hot chocolate.

"Fortunately," added Paul, "there was another one leaving in two hours, but it landed in DC."

"I had just enough juice in my phone to call Mari and tell her to take an Uber out here," Noah went on. "I figured she'd be better off here than waiting for us to pick her up at a strange airport, because God knew how long that would take. That was when I called you to tell you what was going on, but I guess the connection wasn't very good so..." He shrugged.

"This seems to be the pattern with you and last-minute phone calls, Noah," Cici pointed out. She tried to sound stern but didn't quite manage it.

"Anyway, we're all together now," declared Derrick happily, raising his mug. "To the best Christmas surprise ever!"

"Here, here," agreed Paul, and no one had a problem drinking to that.

"Well, I think that's just the sweetest thing I ever heard," declared Freida, unable to keep silent a moment longer. "Don't you think so, Geoff?" Her husband grunted in reply, and she went on cheerily, "And what an adventure! I remember when we were in Germany on that Nordic tour—do you remember that, Geoff? Anyway, there was this little village that looked just like something from a picture postcard. What was the name of it? Oh, never mind, I couldn't pronounce it anyway! But while we were there…"

"Supper's ready." Ida Mae stood at the doorway, hands on hips, looking no more than her usual level of disgruntled. "We got spaghetti and meatballs, turkey and mashed potatoes, and…" She directed her gaze to Lindsay, "Lane cake for dessert."

Bridget said, "Oh, Ida Mae, I forgot about supper! I'm so sorry!"

And Lindsay exclaimed, "Lane cake! Seriously? Oh, my goodness, I can't tell you how I've been craving your Lane cake. I can't wait!"

Frieda declared, "How kind of you to invite us to share your holiday meal with you. Wasn't it kind, Geoff?"

Geoffery took out his earbuds and got to his feet, finishing off his whiskey. "Very hospitable," he agreed gruffly. "Thank you."

There was a moment of stunned silence at the sound of his voice, and then everyone began filing toward the dining room, picking up their conversations. Kevin helped his wife heave herself out of the chair and Lori said, "I can't believe Mariya got herself from the airport all the way out here without speaking a word of English. That's my kind of girl. Tell her that. I think we're going to be friends."

Kevin smiled and caught up with Mariya and Noah, translating what Lori had said into Italian. Mariya smiled gratefully over her shoulder at Lori, then answered when Kevin asked her how she had come to speak Italian.

"She has an uncle in Italy," Kevin explained to the rest of the family when she was finished. "The family scattered during the war and Mariya lived with him for a while. Her parents were loyalists and never encouraged her to learn English, but she's lived and worked all over Europe since she finished school. She speaks Spanish too."

"Oh, I know some Spanish," Derrick said excitedly to Mariya. "*¡Hola! ¡Mi nombre es Derrick!*"

Paul rolled his eyes, "She knows that, Derrick."

Nonetheless, Mariya replied politely, "*Hola, Derrick. Feliz Navidad.*"

"*Feliz Navidad,*" Derrick replied happily, and then his expression fell. "That's all the Spanish I know."

Everyone laughed as they entered the dining room. A fire crackled in the hearth and tapered candles burned in glass hurricane lamps atop the carved mantlepiece. Multicolored glass globes were nestled within a forest of evergreens and white ribbon, and each ornament reflected the dancing light of the candles. The table was set with a white tablecloth and a runner of evergreen branches and pinecones uplit by a net of twinkling white lights. Bridget's best Christmas china and crystal sparkled in the muted light of the teardrop chandelier overhead. A bright red napkin, tied with gold ribbon and a holly sprig, was centered on each plate.

"Oh, boys," Bridget breathed, clasping her hands together, "you did a beautiful job!"

"It's lovely!" exclaimed Frieda. "Isn't it lovely, Geoff?"

"Very festive," he grunted.

From behind them somewhere, Lori said, "Mom?"

"Oh, Lori, come see what Paul and Derrick did," Cici exclaimed, "And bring your phone! We've got to get a picture of us all around the table."

"Shall we just sit anywhere?" said Frieda, "Can I help with serving? Everything smells delicious."

"Mom!" Lori repeated, more demanding now.

They all moved to take a seat and Noah said, "I'm glad everyone's in a good mood because I wanted to ask you all if it would be okay if Mari stayed here with you for a few weeks while I get settled in my new billet. I'd be home every weekend," he added hastily, "and it would only be for a little while."

"We'd love it!" cried Bridget and Cici at the same time, beaming.

Cici added, "Nothing would make us happier. Tell her that." And both Noah and Kevin started talking to Mariya, one in German and one in Italian.

Mariya looked from one to the other in confusion and Noah said, "We've got to settle on one language."

"Mom!"

This time Cici responded to the alarm in her daughter's voice and turned back toward the hallway. Lori was standing a few feet away, looking shocked and scared, staring at the puddle between her feet. "Um, I don't want to gross anybody out," she said, and looked up at her mother helplessly, "but my water broke."

Cici caught the gasp of alarm in her throat that

she knew would only frighten Lori further and came forward quickly to take her arm. "It's okay, sweetie. A little early but perfectly fine. We'll call your doctor, and he'll meet us at the hospital. You've got plenty of time."

"Hospital?" Panic replaced the shock in Lori's eyes. "I can't go to the hospital! I have to get my hair done, and my nails are a mess! I can't have the babies yet," she declared firmly. "I'm not ready."

"Sweetheart," Cici replied gently, "you may have to cancel that appointment at the salon."

Bridget, coming to see what the delay was, immediately assessed the situation and cried, "Kevin! Lori's in labor!"

There was a scraping of chairs and clattering of china as Kevin rushed out of the dining room, followed in short order by everyone else in the room. Kevin put his arm around Lori and started to guide her back toward the parlor. "Okay, baby, everything is fine. We've got this. Just go sit down and rest. I'll get your bag. How far apart are the contractions?"

"I don't know," Lori said impatiently. "Stop making such a fuss. You're embarrassing me. I don't really..." She broke off with a gasp and doubled over, sweat popping out on her forehead. Her knees sagged, and only Kevin's support prevented her from falling. "Not..." she managed in a moment, "very far apart."

Mariya rushed forward and took Lori's other arm, speaking to Kevin in Italian. It took Kevin a moment to translate. "Mariya will stay with you while I get the car. She says breathe. Remember, from Lamaze class?"

"Hurry!" gasped Lori, trying to imitate the slow, deep breaths Mariya modeled for her.

Kevin started for the door, but Noah said, "Dude. You're not going to get very far with that car. Tree down, remember?" He clapped Kevin on the shoulder and moved past him quickly. "I'll get the chainsaw," he said. "Somebody call Farley and tell him to meet me down the road with his tractor."

"I'll do it!" Derrick moved quickly into the kitchen to make the call even as Lori doubled over again with a contraction, grasping her back with one hand and her husband's hand with the other, groaning so loudly it sounded like a roar.

"This is bad," she gasped. Her knuckles were white with the force of gripping Kevin's hand, and her eyes were terrified. "This is really bad. My babies..."

Cici moved close, holding Lori's head to her shoulder with a hand gently across her forehead, trying hard to disguise the anxiety in her own eyes. Mariya pointed with two fingers to Lori's eyes, holding her gaze, demonstrating the quick high breaths she wanted Lori to imitate. "*Bene, bene,*" she said. "*Molto bene.*"

"How far along is she?"

It took Cici a moment to realize that the question had come from Geoffery Stein, and even then she saw no reason to answer him. It was Bridget who said, with a note of desperation in her voice, "Thirty-six weeks."

Geoffery Stein moved forward through the crowd, his eyes narrowed in scrutiny. "That's not too bad," he said, "A lot of twins are delivered at thirty-six weeks. Your babies are going to be fine," he told Lori, "A little over five pounds by the looks of you, and all they're missing is a couple of layers of fat. They'll be okay."

Lori gasped, "You're a doctor?"

"Oh," said Frieda cheerfully, "didn't I mention?"

Geoffery said, "Somebody get an ambulance on its way here. Tell them I want a paramedic onboard, not just EMTs, and I need two preemie incubators. Let's get her upstairs where I can have a look at her."

Cici drew her daughter protectively close, staring at him. "Are you kidding me? Even if you are a doctor, you've been chugging whiskey all day and…"

He gave her a look that had probably sent more than one poor intern scurrying to find a new specialty during his career. "Sipping," he replied coolly. "I've been *sipping* whiskey. I was also the head of obstetrics at Johns Hopkins for twenty-five years and have brought more twins into this world than you're likely to meet in your lifetime. It's up to you, but with or without me those babies are going to be here in little over an hour, I'd say. Premature, home birth, definitely needing someone who's done this a time or two before."

"Mom!" sobbed Lori, clinging to Kevin.

Kevin didn't hesitate. "Thank you, Doctor," Kevin said, breathing hard. "We're glad you're here.

Whatever you say."

Ida Mae looked at Lori, a pleased expression on her face, and gave a sharp nod of her head, "I *told* you it was an angel," she said.

Lori's expression was desperate and confused, "What?"

Ida Mae didn't bother with a reply. She said instead, "I'll go warm up some receiving blankets and towels in the dryer to wrap 'em in when they come out."

"Good idea," said the doctor as she stomped off toward the laundry room, "You." He pointed to Paul. "Go out to the car and bring in my biggest suitcase. My wife will show you which one. It's got my medical bag in it. You." He looked at Mariya as Paul hurried off, tugging Frieda behind him. "You're a nurse, right? You'll assist me. Dad, you translate. Everybody else, stay out of my way. Now, let's get these babies delivered."

~*~

Of course, everyone else did not stay out of his way. It would take more than a doctor's orders to keep Lindsay, Bridget, and Cici out of the birthing room, and even if they had submitted to his will, Lori never would have.

And so it was that at 10:03 and 10:06, respectively, on Christmas Eve, Noelle and Nicholas Gregory-Tyndale were born in an antique four-poster bed on Ladybug Farm. Their entrance into this world was attended by three wise women, a nurse named Mari, and heaven's most unlikely angel. It did not go unnoticed that, in the background, a flock of sheep baaed and rustled softly, and, with the snowstorm now passed, the stars shone on Ladybug Farm more brightly than ever before.

Seven

Christmas Morning

Cici, Bridget, and Lindsay sat in their rocking chairs on the front porch, drinking coffee and eating Lane cake, watching the sun rise over Ladybug Farm. They were wrapped in festive plaid blankets and holiday scarves against the cold; Bridget wore a red knit Santa hat and mittens. Steam rose from their coffee cups and their breaths frosted the air as the distant, misty hills slowly pinkened and became tinged with gold. They had slept less than four hours, but this wasn't the first time a crisis at Ladybug Farm had kept them up all night, and it wouldn't be the last.

The twins, secure in preemie incubators, had been taken to the hospital with their mother by ambulance shortly after midnight. Kevin called to say they had all checked out fine, but the doctor wanted to keep them one more night to be safe. Noah, Mariya and Ida Mae had all gone to bed shortly after that report and were still sleeping. The Steins had missed their flight to Miami, but had managed to book another one leaving at 6:00 that morning. Paul and Derrick had been more than glad to drive them to the airport.

Cici's smile was dreamy as she said, for perhaps the fifth time, "Have you ever seen such beautiful babies?"

Noelle had a feathering of Lori's coppery hair; Nicholas was completely bald. Both had the perfectly formed, delicate features of newborns which, to their grandmothers, appeared to be a perfect melding of both Lori's and Kevin's exceptional good looks.

"They both look just like Kevin," Lindsay remarked, smiling fondly. "Good thing he's so handsome." All of the ladies had gotten to hold the babies briefly before they were taken away, and all of them had fallen instantly in love.

"I think Noelle has Lori's nose," Cici disagreed. "And those sweet little pale eyelashes. Oh, my goodness, so adorable!"

"All babies look like their father for the first three days," Bridget pointed out, rocking contentedly. "So the male parent will bond with them."

Cici looked at her skeptically. "How do you know that?"

Bridget shrugged. "I read it somewhere."

Lindsay said, "I don't understand how Lori could not know she had been in labor all day."

Cici sipped her coffee. "She said the whole pregnancy had been so miserable that a little extra discomfort didn't seem like a big deal."

Bridget shook her head in slow wonder. "Well, that's why girls in their twenties are built for having babies, just like the doctor said. Fewer complications, easier delivery, faster recovery, better outcomes for everybody. Our ancestors knew what they were doing when they got married in their teens."

Cici sighed. "They just seem so young. Lori and Kevin both."

"And Noah," added Lindsay, and the other two agreed.

"It was only a minute ago that he was a skinny kid stealing vegetables from our garden," Bridget said. "How can he be grown up…"

"Speaking *German,*" put in Cici.

"And married!" finished Bridget.

"Tell me about it." Lindsay took another bite of cake. "God, this is good."

Cici smiled at her fondly. Lindsay's auburn hair, now threaded with a little more grey than had been there when she left, was loose around her shoulders and frizzy with the morning damp. There were lines on her face that definitely hadn't been there before. But to the friends she had left behind, she had never looked more beautiful.

Cici said, "You need to get your roots done. Don't they have hairdressers in Florida?"

Lindsay took another bite of cake and shrugged, unconcerned. "Maybe I can take Lori's appointment."

"How did Ida Mae know you were coming?" Bridget asked, trying not to sound hurt. "Did you call her?"

Lindsay looked surprised. "No, of course not.

Why would I do that?"

"You know Ida Mae," Cici told Bridget. "She runs on faith and mule-headedness."

"I guess it was one of those 'if you bake it, they will come' scenarios," Bridget agreed.

After a moment Lindsay said seriously, "I feel bad about not letting you all know what was going on. But it was such short notice, and I didn't want to put you in the position of having to choose between Noah and Lori, and Mari was right—it was a lot of money to spend to just turn around and fly back to the states again, but how could I not go?"

Cici reached across and clasped her hand. "You did the right thing. I wouldn't have left Lori, and anyway, look how well it worked out."

"Talk about your Christmas miracles," Lindsay agreed. She put aside her empty cake plate and picked up her coffee mug, warming her hands around it before taking a sip.

"And that awful man," Bridget said, "sitting there in our living room all day and then turning out to be one of the top OBs in the country. What are the odds?"

Lindsay chuckled, "At Ladybug Farm, pretty damn good."

"You know, you're right," Cici said, grinning. "When things go wrong around here, they go really wrong. But when they go right, it's magic." Her expression sobered as she looked at Lindsay. "Nothing has been right since you left here, Lindsay."

"I know," Lindsay said. She glanced down at the coffee in her mug, and then looked back at the two of them, distress in her eyes. "I'm so sorry. I left you guys alone to run the winery when you needed me most. I left *me* alone when I needed *you* most. I was just so shattered when Dominic died…"

"Oh, honey, I know." Bridget reached across to take Lindsay's hand, her expression full of empathy and compassion. "If it hadn't been for the two of you when Tom died I don't know if I could have made it through."

Lindsay sniffed away tears and smiled sadly. "That's what was so foolish of me. I didn't realize what a gift I had in Ladybug Farm—in you two—until it was gone. And then it was like…" She shook her head helplessly. "I didn't know how to find my way back. Because Ladybug Farm isn't just a place, you know. It's a state of mind."

Cici rested a reassuring hand on Lindsay's shoulder but said nothing, giving her friend the space to finish.

"I missed you guys every day," Lindsay said. "I missed the garden and the winery and the vineyard and the porch and…" she took a breath. "This. Just sitting here being us. I wanted to come home. But it wasn't until that awful mix-up at the airport that I realized I had never left." She brought the hand that held the coffee cup to her chest, over her heart. "Not in here, where it matters."

"Oh, Lindsay," Bridget said softly.

"I mean…" Lindsay paused to take a sip of coffee,

clearing the thickness in her throat, "That kid was willing to send the person he loved most in the world to a bunch of strangers halfway across a country where she didn't even speak the language and he wasn't a bit worried about her. Because he knew he was sending her to a place she'd be welcome, and safe. A place where no one was ever turned away. And then it just came to me that if I wanted to go home..." She shrugged her shoulders a little and looked at them with an expression that was somewhere between shy and embarrassed. "All I had to do was show up."

Without a word, Cici and Bridget left their chairs and wrapped Lindsay in a two-person hug. Lindsay laughed through her misty tears and held the coffee cup away from her body, trying not to spill.

"Best. Christmas. Ever," declared Bridget when she stepped away, and the other two raised their mugs in agreement.

"Although..." Cici gave Lindsay a playful nudge on the shoulder. "I could strangle you for what you put us through. And you're going to have to sleep in the guest room until Kevin and Lori finish renovating the folly."

"Good," declared Lindsay with a nod. "Closer to the babies." She smiled. "You are going to love Mari. I haven't even known her for a week and I'm crazy about her."

"We already love her," Cici assured her. "After what she did for Lori..."

"And how lucky are the twins," added Bridget, "to

have a registered nurse living on the premises when they come home."

"She'll pick up English in no time," Lindsay added, "living with us. As much as we talk, how could she not?"

"Wow," Bridget said, leaning back in her rocker with a pleased expression on her face. "This old house is really filling up."

"I think it's happier that way," observed Cici, and all three of them shared a smile.

They finished their coffee as the sun cleared the hilltops and painted the snowy meadow lavender and gold. Lindsay drained her cup and stood resolutely, "Well," she said, "We've got animals to feed and breakfast to make…"

"And Christmas presents to open," put in Bridget.

"And we'd better get started if we're going to get to the hospital for visiting hours," Lindsay went on. "Are we really giving a party this afternoon?"

"Yes," Cici said, draping an arm around Lindsay's shoulders. "We are. Welcome home, Linds."

Lindsay took a deep breath of the cold morning air. "Best Christmas ever," she said.

And so it was.

Ida Mae's Lane Cake

My mother used to make Lane cakes as Christmas gifts for very special people because, she said, the cake was too expensive and too much trouble to make for anything other than a special occasion. "Eight eggs!" she used to complain. Imagine what she'd say if she had to pay today's prices for them.

I found her handwritten recipe tucked inside a 1941 edition of Mrs. Dull's Cookbook, from which she (like Ida Mae) probably adapted it. For those of you unfamiliar with the venerable Mrs. Dull, she was the kind of cook whose instructions would read, "Make a white layer cake" – with the full confidence that you, the reader, would know exactly how to do that. For this reason, there are quite a few variations on the original Lane cake recipe. My mother, for example, used a butter cream frosting; others, like Ida Mae, use a boiled, or 7-minute, frosting. Both are delicious!

What follows is part Mother, part Mrs. Dull, and all Ida Mae. Enjoy!

Lane Cake

For the Cake:

8 egg whites
1 cup butter, softened
2 cups sugar
1 cup milk
4 cups flour
3 teaspoons baking powder

¼ teaspoon salt
1 teaspoon vanilla

Preheat oven to 350 degrees.

Beat butter and sugar together until creamy. Add egg whites and vanilla and mix well. Sift together dry ingredients and add alternately with milk. Pour into three 9-in layers and bake at 350 for 20-25 minutes or until a wooden pick inserted in the center comes out clean. (*Times may vary! This is an old recipe*). Cool layers completely.

For Filling:

8 egg yolks
1 cup sugar
½ cup butter
1 cup raisins
1 cup pecans
4-8 ounces (depending upon your taste) red wine, brandy, or liquor of choice
1 teaspoon vanilla extract

Beat yolks, add other ingredients and mix well. Cook in a double boiler over simmering water until thick. Spread filling between layers. May be refrigerated overnight to allow flavors to meld. Frost with boiled (7-minute) frosting (below) or a white buttercream. Keep in mind that the boiled frosting will break down within a couple of days, so this cake is best served within 24 hours of frosting.

7 Minute Frosting

1 ½ cups white sugar
½ cup water
2 egg whites
½ teaspoon salt
1 tablespoon light corn syrup
1 teaspoon vanilla extract

Combine sugar, water, egg whites, salt, corn syrup, and vanilla in the top of a double boiler. Beat all ingredients for about one minute before placing the bowl or pan over the heat.
Place over rapidly boiling water; beat at high speed until the mixture forms soft peaks. (This may take longer than 7 minutes).
Transfer the frosting mixture to a large bowl; continue to beat until the mixture is thick and cool enough to spread.

~*~

Acknowledgements

This story belongs to all those readers who have kept in touch with me so faithfully all these years, who have shared with me their favorite things about Ladybug Farm, and who have so generously encouraged me with their own hopes for future books. I couldn't possibly list them all by name. In particular, I would like to thank Allyson Krauel, who, while recovering from a serious illness, dreamed of Ladybug Farm and took the time to write me a long letter describing how the characters lived on in her imagination. It was she who inspired the idea for Mariya, who I think we can all agree was a pivotal part of this story. I hope I have done her justice!

About The Author

Donna Ball is the author of over 100 books under a variety of pseudonyms. Though she has been published in virtually every genre, she is best known for her work in women's fiction, mystery and suspense. Her novels have been translated into multiple languages and published around the world. Her most popular series are the award-winning Raine Stockton Dog Mystery series, the Dogleg Island Mystery series, The Blood River Mystery series, and the Ladybug Farm series. All are available now in paperback in bookstores everywhere, as audiobook downloads, and in digital format for your e-reader.

Donna lives in the heart of the Blue Ridge Divide in a restored Victorian barn which was the inspiration for the bestselling *A YEAR ON LADYBUG FARM.* She spends her spare time hiking, painting, and enjoying canine sports with her three dogs. You can reach her at www.donnaball.net.

The Ladybug Farm series
For every woman who ever had a dream… or a friend

A Year on Ladybug Farm
At Home on Ladybug Farm
Love Letters from Ladybug Farm
Christmas on Ladybug Farm: A Novella
Recipes from Ladybug Farm
Vintage Ladybug Farm
A Wedding on Ladybug Farm
A Gift from Ladybug Farm: A Novella
And
The Hummingbird House
Christmas at the Hummingbird House
The Hummingbird House Presents

More from Donna Ball

The Blood River Mystery Series

UNFIXABLE: A Buck Lawson Mystery

Former sheriff Buck Lawson leaves the mountains of North Carolina to take a job as police chief of the small South Georgia town of Mercy, and soon finds himself in over his head. For one thing, his predecessor has been murdered...

WELCOME TO BETHLEHEM: *A Buck Lawson Short Novella*

Police chief Buck Lawson wants his first Christmas in his new hometown of Mercy, Georgia, to be a memorable one, both for his family and the police officers under his command. But while preparing to host the traditional police department Christmas party, Buck's home is burglarized by a Middle Eastern man who may be connected to far more violent crimes. As the investigation unfolds and unsettling connections to the past come to light, Buck fears this Christmas will be memorable for all the wrong reasons.

Also Available in the Holiday Anthology **DECK THE HALLS**

Unstoppable: A Buck Lawson Mystery

With the Fourth of July coming up and the Mercy police force already stretched to its limit, police chief Buck Lawson investigates a fraud complaint that leads him to a missing newborn and a terrified, runaway mother. At the same time, the skeletal remains of two young boys are discovered buried on the property of a prominent citizen. When a young woman is murdered, the web of secrecy protecting Mercy begins to unravel, revealing a network of illegal activity that has gone undeterred for decades.

The Raine Stockton Dog Mystery Series
Books in Order

SMOKY MOUNTAIN TRACKS

A child has been kidnapped and abandoned in the mountain wilderness. Her only hope is Raine Stockton and her young, untried tracking dog Cisco...

RAPID FIRE

Raine and Cisco are brought in by the FBI to track a terrorist ...a terrorist who just happens to be Raine's old boyfriend.

GUN SHY

Raine rescues a traumatized service dog, and soon begins to suspect he is the only witness to a murder.

BONE YARD

Cisco digs up human remains in Raine's back yard, and mayhem ensues. Could this be evidence of a serial killer, a long-unsolved mass murder, or something even more sinister... and closer to home?

SILENT NIGHT

It's Christmastime in Hansonville, N.C., and Raine and Cisco are on the trail of a missing teenager. But when a newborn is abandoned in the manger of the town's living nativity and Raine walks in on what appears to be the scene of a murder, the holidays take a very dark turn for everyone concerned.

THE DEAD SEASON

Raine and Cisco take a job leading a wilderness hike for troubled teenagers, and soon find themselves trapped on a mountainside in a blizzard... with a killer.

ALL THAT GLITTERS: A Holiday Short Story e book

Raine looks back on how she and Cisco met and solved their first crime in this Christmas Cozy short story. Sold separately as an e-book or bundled with the print edition of HIGH IN TRIAL.

HIGH IN TRIAL

A carefree weekend turns deadly when Raine and Cisco travel to the South Carolina low country for an agility competition

DOUBLE DOG DARE

A luxury Caribbean vacation sounds like just the ticket for over-worked, over-stressed Raine Stockton and her happy go lucky canine companion Cisco. But even in paradise trouble finds them, and when someone she loves is threatened Raine must use every resource at her command to track down a killer before it's too late.

HOME OF THE BRAVE

There's a new dog in town, and Raine and Cisco find themselves unexpectedly upstaged by a flashy K-9 addition to the sheriff's department. But when things go terribly wrong at a mountain camp for kids and dogs over the Fourth of July weekend, Raine and Cisco need all the help they can get to save themselves, and those they love.

DOG DAYS

Raine takes in a lost English Cream Golden Retriever, and the search for her owner leads Raine and Cisco into the hands of a killer. Readers will enjoy a treasure hunt for the titles of all ten of the Raine Stockton Dog Mysteries hidden in this special tenth anniversary release!

LAND OF THE FREE

On a routine search and rescue mission Raine Stockton and her golden retriever Cisco stumble onto something they were never meant to find, and are plunged into a nightmare of murder, corruption and intrigue as figures from her past re-emerge to threaten everything Raine holds dear.

DEADFALL

Hollywood comes to Hanover County, and Raine and Cisco get caught up in the drama when a series of mishaps on the set lead to murder.

THE DEVIL'S DEAL

Raine takes temporary custody of what may well be the most valuable dog in the world, but when lives are at stake she is forced to make an unthinkable choice.

MURDER CREEK

Raine and Cisco rescue a dog who is locked in a hot car in a remote Smoky Mountain park... and subsequently discover the owner of that car drowned in the creek only a few dozen yards away. Was it an accident, or was it murder?

ANGELS IN THE SNOW: *A Raine Stockton Short Novella*

 While preparing for the annual Dog Daze Christmas party, Raine leaves on a secret Christmas errand and becomes trapped in a blizzard. Injured and alone, with a desperate criminal on the loose, a surprising canine hero comes to her rescue. But is it all a product of her imagination, or a genuine Christmas miracle?

Also available in in **DECK THE HALLS**: A HOLIDAY MYSTERY ANTHOLOGY

THE JUDGES DAUGHTER

In this pivotal fifteenth book in the ground-breaking Raine

Stockton Dog Mystery Series, the death of an old friend leaves Raine Stockton with an unwanted inheritance, an old wound reopened, and the most challenging mystery of her life.

DEAD MAN'S TRAIL

Deep in the heart of the Smoky Mountains there a thousand things that will kill you... and one of them is human.

Raine and Cisco agree to help instruct a group of executives at a survival training camp. On a routine exercise, the group becomes stranded in the wilderness with an ice storm moving in. With all communications disabled, they are completely cut off from the modern world and being hunted by a man to whom killing is a way of life. As one by one their members are picked off, the survivors must rely on Raine and Cisco to lead them to safety. But as the killer draws ever closer, even Raine is no longer sure where safety lies.

Don't miss this thrilling first installment in The Hunter Saga, Raine and Cisco's most harrowing adventure yet!

~*~

The Dogleg Island Mystery Series

FLASH

Dogleg Island Mystery #1

Almost two years ago the sleepy little community of Dogleg Island was the scene of one of the most brutal crimes in Florida history. The only eye witnesses were Flash, a border collie puppy, and a police officer. Now the trial of the century is about to begin. The defendant, accused of slaughtering his parents in their beach home, maintains his innocence. The top witnesses for the prosecution are convinced he is lying. But only Flash knows the truth. And with another murder to solve and a monster storm on the way, the truth may come to late… for all of them.

THE SOUND OF RUNNING HORSES

Dogleg Island Mystery #2

A family outing takes a dark turn when Flash, Aggie and Grady discover a body on deserted Wild Horse Island, and the evidence appears to point to someone they know—and trust.

FLASH OF BRILLIANCE

Dogleg Island Mystery #3

Aggie, Flash and Grady look forward to their first Christmas as a family until a homicide hit-and-run exposes a crime syndicate, and dark shadows from the past return to haunt their future.

PIECES OF EIGHT

Dogleg Island Mystery #4

A deadly explosion at an archeological dig on Dogleg Island plunges police chief Aggie Malone and her canine partner Flash into a dark mystery from the past, while on the other side of the bridge, Deputy Sheriff Ryan Grady stumbles onto the site of a mass murder. As the investigation unfolds, Aggie and Grady see that the two cases are related, but only Flash knows how…and by whom.

FLASH IN THE DARK

Dogleg Island Mystery #5

Flash discovers an abandoned child on the beach, and the subsequent attempt to identify her leads to a secret organization with a plan for revenge that has been decades in the making. Unless Aggie, Grady and Flash can stop it they risk losing everything the love… even Dogleg Island itself.

THE GOOD SHEPHERD: *A Dogleg Island Short Novella*

A missing infant, a holiday pageant, and a priest determined to do the right thing no matter what the cost all come together to present Dogleg Island police chief Aggie Malone and her canine assistant Flash with one of their most unusual cases yet. When a routine call escalates into a kidnapping on the eve of the annual Dogleg Island Police Department holiday open house, Flash and Aggie are held hostage by a desperate man whose only chance for redemption may be the grace of the holiday season.

Also Available in **DECK THE HALLS**: A HOLIDAY MYSTERY ANTHOLOGY

FLASH OF FIRE:

Dogleg Island Mystery #6

Ecoterrorists threaten Dogleg Island, and the only person who can save the island from catastrophe may be more dangerous than the terrorists themselves.

~*~

Spine-chilling suspense by Donna Ball

SHATTERED

A missing child, a desperate call for help in the middle of the night... is this a cruel hoax, or the work of a maniacal serial killer who is poised to strike again?

NIGHT FLIGHT

She's an innocent woman who knows too much. Now she's fleeing through the night without a weapon and without a phone, and her only hope for survival is a cop who's willing to risk his badge—and his life—to save her.

SANCTUARY

They came to the peaceful, untouched mountain wilderness of Eastern Tennessee seeking an escape from the madness of modern life. But when they built their luxury homes in the heart of virgin forest they did not realize that something was there before them... something ancient and horrible; something that will make them believe that monsters are real.

EXPOSURE

Everyone has secrets, but when talk show host Jessamine Cray's stalker begins to use her past to terrorize her, no one is safe ... not her family, her friends, her coworkers, and especially not Jess herself.

RENEGADE by Donna Boyd

Enter a world of dark mystery and intense passion, where human destiny is controlled by a species of powerful, exotic creatures. Once they ruled the Tundra, now they rule Wall Street. Once they fought with teeth and claws, now they fight with wealth and power. And only one man can stop them... if he dares.